"You don't remember, do you?"

Sidonie blinked again, derailed by the unexpected question. "Remember? Remember what?"

"How you told me that if you had not married by the time your thirtieth birthday came around, then you would marry me."

A flush of heat swept through her, closely followed by a tide of ice, and all the cool demands she'd been going to make, such as what Khalil was doing here and why, abruptly vanished from her head.

That night in Soho, that's what he was talking about. The night she didn't want to remember. Not the words that had come out of her mouth that had driven him away, and definitely not the stained napkin she'd pulled out from under her cocktail glass and used to write down the most ridiculous promise. A promise she'd made him sign.

Three Ruthless Kings

Romance cannot be ruled...

At university, royal friends Galen Kouros, Khalil ibn Amir al-Nazari and Augustine Solari were known as the wicked princes, causing mayhem wherever they went! Now they're the three ruthless kings, each responsible for a whole nation, wielding more power than many could comprehend.

But even from their gilded thrones, there is one thing these kings are about to learn they cannot control...

Solace Ashworth is back and there's one thing she wants from Galen...their son! Read on in:

Wed for Their Royal Heir

Khalil hasn't forgotten the contract Sidonie Sullivan signed years ago. Now he's about to make her his queen! Read on in:

Her Vow to Be His Desert Queen

Both available now!

And look out for Augustine's story, where Winifred Scott is rumored to be carrying the king's heir!

Pregnant with Her Royal Boss's Baby

Coming soon!

Jackie Ashenden

HER VOW TO BE HIS DESERT QUEEN

ISBN-13: 978-1-335-73946-9

Her Vow to Be His Desert Queen

Harlequin Enterprises ULC
22 Adelaide St. West, 41st Floor
Toronto, Ontario M5H 4E3, Canada
www.Harlequin.com

Printed in U.S.A.

Recycling programs
for this product may
not exist in your area.

Jackie Ashenden writes dark, emotional stories with alpha heroes who've just gotten the world to their liking only to have it blown apart by their kick-ass heroines. She lives in Auckland, New Zealand, with her husband, the inimitable Dr. Jax, two kids and two rats. When she's not torturing alpha males and their gutsy heroines, she can be found drinking chocolate martinis, reading anything she can lay her hands on, wasting time on social media or being forced to go mountain biking with her husband. To keep up-to-date with Jackie's new releases and other news, sign up to her newsletter at jackieashenden.com.

Books by Jackie Ashenden

Harlequin Presents

The Innocent Carrying His Legacy
The Wedding Night They Never Had
The Innocent's One-Night Proposal
The Maid the Greek Married

Three Ruthless Kings

Wed for Their Royal Heir

Pregnant Princesses

Pregnant by the Wrong Prince

Rival Billionaire Tycoons

A Diamond for My Forbidden Bride
Stolen for My Spanish Scandal

Visit the Author Profile page
at Harlequin.com for more titles.

To my process. Without which I wouldn't have had to write the beginning of this book three times. Thanks for nothing!

CHAPTER ONE

SIDONIE SULLIVAN STARED, irritated, at the half-pint of lager and packet of pork scratchings sitting on the table in front of her.

'Happy birthday, Sid.' Derek, who was sitting in the booth seat opposite and who'd bought her both the half-pint and the pork scratchings, smiled. 'I know it's not much, but I've got dinner booked at Giovanni's and that's a bit special, don't you think?'

Sidonie smiled back, forcing away the slight twinge of impatience. 'Thanks, Derek. This is… lovely.'

It *was* lovely. Derek was an old school friend, and it was very nice of him to take her out for a birthday dinner, but he was part of a life she'd left behind five years ago when she'd moved to London. A life that didn't bear any resemblance to the life she had now, and one she didn't particularly want to return to.

She was only here in Blackchurch, the little Oxfordshire village she'd grown up in, to pay a visit to her aunt, and then she'd be returning to London the next day, and quite frankly she couldn't wait. Blackchurch was small and insular, and she'd never felt at home there. Plus, Aunt May had always been awful, and time hadn't made her any less so. It was more a duty visit than anything else, since May wasn't in good health and had no one else to check on her.

Not that Sidonie could afford time away from the children's charity she'd started five years earlier. The charity was getting bigger every day, providing opportunities for disadvantaged kids all over the country, and she had plans to take it to Europe too, then maybe the rest of the world. There was always so much to do.

So much so that she'd forgotten it was her birthday until Derek, on hearing she was back for a visit—the village telegraph was apparently very much alive and well—had knocked on her aunt's door and asked Sidonie out.

She hadn't wanted to go—she had emails to answer, a report to write, and a couple of phone calls to make—but Derek had been insistent, and Aunt May, who hadn't been all that thrilled to be visited anyway, had wanted to be left alone to 'watch her shows'. So Sidonie had reluctantly agreed. She couldn't recall the last time she or anyone else had actually celebrated her birthday—certainly her aunt never had—so it had been very nice of Derek to remember.

He *would have.*

The thought came out of nowhere, startling her. How strange for her to think of *him,* after all this time. Not that he was relevant at all right now. He'd left England five years ago and the only communication she'd had since then had been a terse email telling her it would be best if they didn't contact each other again.

So she hadn't. She'd put *him* firmly out of her mind that day, so why she was thinking about him now was anyone's guess.

She smiled determinedly at Derek because, while she wasn't attracted to him in the least, he was a nice man who'd wanted to do something lovely for her and she appreciated it.

'So, Sid,' Derek began.

But she never found out what he'd been going to say because at that moment the pub door banged open and in strode six powerful-looking men wearing black suits, sunglasses, and earpieces. One went straight to the bar to talk to the publican, while the others went systematically around the room getting people to their feet and herding them out of the door.

Sidonie frowned.

'What's going on?' Derek threw a puzzled look in the direction of the black-suited men. 'Is this a movie or something?'

Good question. The men seemed to be some kind of security team, though why on earth they'd be here, in this obscure English pub, she had no idea.

Then quite suddenly, all six of the black-suited men snapped to attention, one of them announcing something in a lyrical language that definitely wasn't

English. The other five repeated it like a mantra and then another man strolled into the pub.

And Sidonie's whole world slowed down and stopped.

He was very, *very* tall, with the kind of wide shoulders and broad chest a Greek god would have been proud of, and he moved with all the grace of an apex predator. Which he most certainly was. His face was all sharp planes and angles, with the fierce beauty of a bird of prey, and his sharp black gaze missed nothing.

His dark, handmade suit was immaculate, his white cotton shirt serving only to highlight the burnished bronze of his skin, and he wore power and arrogance as if both had been tailor-made specifically for him.

There was nothing about him that was not beautiful.

In one hand he held a small but perfectly frosted chocolate cupcake with a candle in the centre and in the other a red balloon.

Sidonie felt as if her heart had stopped beating.

It was *him*. It was Khalil ibn Amir al Nazari. The man who'd once been her best friend in all the world. The man she'd fallen in love with and who'd walked away from her five years earlier, leaving her standing alone in a snowy street in London.

She hadn't seen him since.

She'd met him when they were both students at Oxford. He'd been one of the 'Wicked Princes', a group of three young royals infamous among the colleges of the university town. Galen Kouros, Prince of Kalithera. Augustine Solari, Prince of Isavere. And him. Khalil, heir to the throne of Al Da'ira, a small but very rich country near the Red Sea.

She hadn't paid much attention to the Wicked Princes—she was quiet and studious, and on a scholarship too, so she had no time for parties or any of the wild shenanigans they and their friends got up to.

Then one day, she'd been working at her part-time job stacking books in one of the college libraries, when a deep, dark male voice had peremptorily demanded her help, and when she'd turned around she'd found him standing there. Khalil, arrogant and so totally mesmerising she'd lost the power of speech. He'd repeated his question, even more arrogant and demanding than he'd been the first time, and she'd been so shocked and surprised that she'd laughed at him. Of course, then she'd felt terrible, and had apologised, but first he'd stared at her as if she was the most fascinating thing he'd ever seen. Then he'd told her that her apology wasn't necessary and that he should be the one apologising, since he'd been very rude.

That had been the start of their friendship, a strange meeting of opposites: the Prince and the scholarship girl. It shouldn't have worked. She'd been brought up by her working-class aunt, while he'd been brought up a prince. She was quiet and studious, while he was wild, going to all the parties with his friends, and barely attending lectures.

Yet they'd been drawn to each other and had become best friends, staying in contact even after they'd left university.

Or rather, they'd been best friends up until five years ago, when the disaster of that night in Soho had happened, and she'd said those things she should never have said, and he'd walked away from her. Then, a month later, she'd got that email from him telling her that he had no plans to return to England, and that it would better if she didn't contact him again. He hadn't given a reason why.

Not that he had to explain. She knew why.

He'd broken her heart that day, but she refused to let it be a mortal blow. Instead, she changed, armouring herself, guarding herself. Becoming a different person. A person who didn't give her heart so readily to someone who didn't want it.

She never thought she'd see him again, yet here he was, standing arrogantly in the middle of the pub like a god manifesting before his mortal worshippers, staring around until his black gaze finally settled on her.

All the breath left her lungs. There seemed to be no air anywhere in the room.

Derek started to say something but Khalil was already stalking towards them, the balloon bobbing with every step. It would have been amusing if the expression on his beautiful face hadn't been suddenly so utterly intent.

Her heart began to race. She was a rabbit caught in the headlights of a car, unable to move, unable to look away.

Five years since she'd seen him and he was still every bit the same mesmerising, utterly compelling man she remembered from their last meeting in London.

He'd been in England on a state visit, and they'd arranged to meet at a too-loud bar in Soho. That was when he'd broken the news to her that his father had died, and he had to return to Al Da'ira to take the throne. He wouldn't be back for some time, he'd said. Probably years. His country was in trouble, and he needed to be there to help it through the transition in ruler.

She understood. His father had been a terrible king and Khalil's presence was required for the nation's stability. But she'd also been upset at the thought of not seeing him for so long, and had had a couple more Cosmopolitans than she should have, making him promise all kinds of ridiculous things.

But it hadn't been until the time had come to say goodbye, as they'd stood outside the bar in the falling snow, that she'd made that terrible, costly mistake.

In a fit of wild emotion she'd told him she loved him, and as soon as the words were out of her mouth she knew she'd said the wrong thing. Because shock had flared in his dark eyes and then his beautiful face had shuttered, becoming as cold as the snow falling all around them.

He'd been gentle, prying her fingers from where they clutched at his coat, but he hadn't said a single thing in response.

He'd simply turned on his heel and walked away,

leaving her standing there alone, her heart slowly shattering to pieces in her chest.

She'd cried all night into her pillow after he'd gone, castigating herself for ruining things between them, because she quite clearly had. He'd never given her any indication that he felt anything for her but friendship, so why she'd told him that she loved him she still couldn't understand. It had been the Cosmopolitans maybe, or the stupid promise she'd written on a serviette and made him sign. Or perhaps it had been simply that raw rush of emotion as she'd stood there looking up in his dark eyes and watching the snow settle in his black hair.

She should have known better than to say it out loud, though. Her aunt had always told her she was too needy and demanding, and it was obvious from Khalil's response to her that he thought so too. Which was confirmed a few weeks later when his email had arrived to tell her it would be easier on both of them if she didn't contact him again.

So she didn't. By that stage the charity she'd started up after leaving university was gathering steam and she'd moved to London, and it was easy to immerse herself in work. Easy to bury the remains of her broken heart and become someone else. Someone with purpose and determination and steel. A strong woman. A woman who didn't cry into her pillow all night because of some man. A woman who needed nothing and no one.

Now, though, despite all of that, her heartbeat was racing the way it always did whenever he was around, and she fought to find the steely determination that had helped her drive her charity to the top, meeting his dark gaze steadily.

It didn't matter that he was back five years after he'd broken her heart.

It didn't matter at all.

'Khalil,' she began, pleased with how level her voice sounded. 'What are—?'

'Get out,' Khalil interrupted. And there was no doubt about who he was talking to, because Derek was on his feet and through the door before Sidonie could get another word out.

Anger prickled over her skin.

So here he was, presumably for her, since there was no other reason for him to be in Blackchurch, having tracked her down after five years of silence. And the first words out of his mouth weren't 'I'm sorry, Sidonie, for walking away'. Or 'I'm sorry for telling you not to contact me again'. No, they were 'Get out' to the one man who'd actually had the decency to take her for a birthday treat.

She wanted to tell him how rude he was and how dared he come here and frighten away the first date she'd had in years? But that would make her sound angry with him. That would make her sound as if she cared, and she didn't.

She was over him. She'd been over him for years.

So she said nothing as he calmly slid into the booth, taking Derek's place as if the poor man hadn't ever been there. He deposited the cupcake on the table before holding the balloon out to her. 'Happy birthday, Sidonie,' he said in his dark, deep voice, as if he'd only been away a couple of days and not five years.

For a second she had no idea what response to make, her brain still trying to process the fact that he was here, in England, in this pub, let alone that he'd just wished her happy birthday as if they were still friends. Then, when the reality of his presence finally hit, despite all her assurances to herself, those hot, angry words filled her mouth anyway, and she had to swallow them down to stop them from coming out.

Shouting at him was pointless. It didn't matter that he'd broken off their friendship as if it had meant nothing. As if *she* meant nothing.

It didn't matter how he treated her; she didn't care. She was successful and happy and didn't need him any more.

Ignoring the anger that sat hot and burning in the pit of her stomach, she also forced down the betraying leap of joy that tightened around her heart. And gave him a cool, measuring look. 'Khalil. This is a surprise. I wasn't expecting to see you, obviously. But I was actually in the middle of a date.' Really, he should know he'd interrupted something. She hadn't been sitting around all these years just waiting for him.

Those dark, winged brows arrowed down. 'A date? With whom?'

It seemed some things hadn't changed. The Oxford colleges had had their fair share of arrogant people, but Khalil's arrogance was really something else. So far, so prince, she'd thought. Yet even his two friends, Galen and Augustine, who were also princes and whom she'd met very briefly a couple of times, weren't as arrogant as he was.

Then she'd found out that Al Da'ira was an absolute monarchy where the rulers were viewed as semi-divine, and their word was law. In that context his arrogance had made sense, though she hadn't put up with it. He'd liked that about her, or so he'd said. He liked that she treated him as an ordinary person, not a prince.

Except the man sitting opposite her now didn't look like an ordinary person. He didn't look like the friend she remembered either, the intense, brooding young man he'd once been. He'd been like a stormy, dark sea, she'd often thought back then. Full of complex, dangerous currents, and yet when the sun shone through the water there was such lightness and aching beauty. His rare smiles. His compassion. His deeply hidden, wry sense of humour.

None of that was in evidence now, though. The lines of his face were hard and set and cold. He wasn't the sea any more. He was the rock that lay at the bottom of it.

'It was a birthday date,' she explained coolly. 'With Derek.'

'Derek?' Khalil glanced around. 'I see no Derek.'

'No. Because you just rudely ordered him out of the pub.'

'Him? He was in my way.' Khalil gestured insistently with the balloon. 'Take it.'

Her heart gave a tiny jolt that he'd remembered, but she'd told herself she wasn't going to let anything he did or said mean anything, so again she ignored it.

You want it to mean something, though.

No. No, she absolutely did not. She'd got rid of the last remaining feelings she had for him years ago. And if her heart ached and she felt breathless on seeing him now, it was only shock. Nothing more.

However, it seemed silly not to take the balloon, so she reached for it. Only to fight yet another jolt, this time physically as his fingers brushed hers and a familiar spark of electricity leapt between them.

She still remembered the first time she'd felt it, the night Khalil had thrown her a birthday party for her twenty-first. She'd never had a party before, because her aunt had never celebrated her birthday, still less a surprise party.

It had been the most wonderful night. She didn't have many friends, but he'd invited all of them, plus his own bigger, wilder crowd. There had been lots of music and laughter, and dancing. There had been balloons. There had been a cake. Everyone had sung her 'Happy Birthday', and she'd nearly cried because it had been so lovely.

Her first birthday party ever and it had been a huge success.

Much later that night, Khalil had pulled her into his arms and danced with her, and she'd become aware, all at once, of his warmth. The hard-muscled plane of his chest. His scent. She'd always thought of him as beautiful, dazzling even. But that was the night she'd realised she wanted him.

An echo of that old longing hit her now, making her hand jerk and the balloon bob violently in response. Luckily, he didn't seem to notice.

'Thank you,' she said, with what she hoped was some degree of calm. 'Both for the balloon and the cupcake. But really, you were inexcusably rude to Derek and I should go and make sure—'

'I will deal with it,' Khalil interrupted with the same arrogance she remembered from years ago. Or maybe not the same. There was a hard edge to it now that hadn't been there before.

He turned his head and instantly one of his men was there. He issued a curt command in the lyrical Arabic dialect of his home country, and the man darted away.

Sidonie frowned. 'What did you say to him?'

'I told him to go and find your Derek and pay him a suitable amount of money for the inconvenience of ending your date early.' Khalil smiled, his teeth flashing white against his bronzed skin, but his black eyes remained sharp as obsidian. 'Do not worry.'

That smile wasn't the same either. There was no warmth in it at all. A tiger's smile.

He is not the man you knew. Not any more.

'So, what are you doing here?' she asked in the most neutral voice possible, repressing the odd shiver that went through her. 'Apart from being terribly rude to a friend of mine, of course. I didn't know you were in the country.' She wasn't going to point out exactly how long it had been since he'd last contacted her, because naturally she hadn't been keeping track.

Khalil didn't reply. Instead, he frowned down at the cupcake. Then abruptly he held out his hand and one of the men in black suits sprang over and put a lighter in it. Khalil didn't look at him, proceeding to light the candle on her cupcake before holding his hand out again so the same man could take the lighter from it. Then he leaned back in the booth seat, powerful arms resting across the back of it, and fixed her with an intense stare.

'Blow,' he ordered.

Sidonie blinked. 'What?'

'The candle.' He didn't take his gaze from hers. 'Blow it out.'

Another shiver whispered over her skin as memories slowly filtered through her head. Of the way he'd used to look at her, the way he was doing now. Intense and focused, as if what she had to say was vital and he didn't want to miss a word.

He'd always had the ability to make her feel she was interesting and special, as if what she said was worth hearing, an addictive thing to the kid who'd lost her parents at eight and had to go and live with her father's cold and unemotional sister. Aunt May, who'd made it very clear to Sidonie that she was looking after her only as a duty to her brother. That Sidonie was an imposition she hadn't looked for and didn't want, but took anyway out of the goodness of her heart.

It's still addictive...

No, absolutely not. She wasn't going to fall into that trap again. She was a successful businesswoman with a charity dedicated to helping disadvantaged children, and she didn't need his or anyone else's validation, still less his. She'd graduated from Oxford with honours, had put all her drive and determination into making a difference to orphaned children's lives, and she wasn't lonely these days. She was secure and confident in herself, no matter how first her aunt and then Khalil's abandonment had made her feel otherwise.

Shoving her physical reaction to him away, Sidonie let out a silent breath and held his gaze. Back when they'd been friends, she'd never let him get away with his high-handed behaviour, and she certainly wasn't going to let him get away with it now.

She raised a brow. 'Only if you sing "Happy Birthday".'

'Very well,' he said and without hesitation began to sing, his deep voice making each and every word sound like an intimate caress. 'Happy birthday to you, happy birthday to you, happy birthday dear Sidonie, happy birthday to you.'

She shouldn't have told him to sing. There were too many memories associated with him singing her 'Happy Birthday'. Memories of the night he'd danced with her, and she didn't need those in her head.

'Now blow,' he ordered once he'd finished.

Arguing about blowing out a candle was ridiculous, and after all, it *was* her birthday, so she leaned forward and blew, watching as the flame flickered and went out.

Then she straightened. 'So, I guess I should be honoured that you—'

'You don't remember, do you?'

Sidonie blinked again, derailed by the unexpected question. 'Remember? Remember what?'

'How you told me that if you had not married by the time your thirtieth birthday came around, then you would marry me.'

A flush of heat swept through her, closely followed by a tide of ice, and all the cool demands she'd been going to make, such as what he was doing here and why, abruptly vanished from her head.

That night in Soho, that was what he was talking about. The night she didn't want to remember. Not the words that had come out of her mouth, that had driven him away, and definitely not the stained serviette she'd pulled out from under her cocktail glass and used to write down the most ridiculous promise. A promise she'd made him sign.

Heat worked its way up her throat, over her jaw and into her cheeks, and there was nothing she could do to stop it. The curse of being a redhead meant fine white skin that betrayed every single emotion. And, of course, he'd see it too. He missed nothing.

'It was on that last night in London,' Khalil went on smoothly, still watching her. Clearly, he had no problem with remembering it. 'My father had just died and we met for a drink in Soho. I told you I didn't know when I could come back for a visit, so you made me promise to return at least by the time you were thirty. You also promised that if you weren't married by then, you'd marry me.'

The heat felt like a fire now, burning her skin, the awful, awful memories of that night and how she'd humiliated herself so clear in her head. They'd talked of Al Da'ira and all the changes Khalil would make now he was King, changes he'd often discussed with her when they'd been at university. They'd both been passionate about wanting to make people's lives better, she already with plans for a charity, he with his plans for when he took the crown.

He'd told her that night that he would obviously need to marry at some stage and that was when she'd got it into her head that he could marry her. It had been the cocktails making her brave, the powerful feeling in her heart and the fact that he was leaving that had driven her to write it down as a promise. A vow.

It seemed so stupid now. So naïve. So…desperate. She wasn't that woman any longer and hadn't been for years.

So she ignored the blush burning in her cheeks and stared back into his dark eyes. 'Oh, right, yes. And wasn't there some kind of…?' She pretended to grasp for the memory. 'I wrote it down and made you sign something, didn't I?'

If he knew she was lying, he gave no sign. 'Indeed.' Reaching into the breast pocket of his suit jacket, he withdrew a dog-eared piece of paper. 'I think this is what you are talking about.' He laid the paper down gently beside the cupcake and unfolded it, his gaze somehow growing even sharper.

She couldn't help it—she glanced down at it. A stained serviette still with the slightly pink ring mark from her Cosmo, and her handwriting, untidy and rushed.

Khalil said nothing.

Half reluctant, half in the grip of a kind of horrified fascination, she picked it up and yes, there it was, all her embarrassing need writ large in black ballpoint. And there, damningly, at the end, her own scrawled signature beside his, because she knew she'd never change her mind. Never in a million years…

She stared at the serviette for a long minute. Then she did what she always did whenever he did or said something preposterous.

She laughed.

Khalil waited patiently for Sidonie to stop laughing, watching her green eyes light up and her pale, creamy, freckle-dotted skin flush.

He remembered that laugh. Remembered the way it lit her up inside. Remembered how it had used to make him laugh too, which he'd always found curious, as he'd never had anything to laugh about.

It had been so long since he'd seen her. So long since he'd heard that laugh. So long since he'd laughed at anything himself. He'd almost forgotten how.

If he'd still been her friend, he would have laughed

too. But he wasn't her friend, not any more, and so he only looked at her, drinking in the sight.

She was different. He'd been able to tell the moment he'd walked in.

Her fire-red hair was piled up on top of her head in her usual bun—he remembered her sticking a pen in it to hold it in place when they'd used to study together—but it wasn't messy the way he remembered it. It was neat and tidy, not a hair out of place. No stray curls falling down around her ears and the back of her neck, softening her lovely, heart-shaped face.

She wasn't in one of the colourful dresses she'd always worn either. Tonight she was in severe black trousers and a crisp white shirt, a black jacket folded neatly on the seat beside her.

She didn't smile at him, not the way she'd used to. Those green eyes of hers had been nothing but hostile ever since he'd sat down, and even the way she was laughing right now had an edge to it that held no amusement.

Are you surprised? After you ignored her for five years?

He hadn't ignored her. He'd cut her off completely. Which made coming back to England a gamble, but one he'd been willing to make.

Yet he'd been away a long time and, with the memory of their last meeting echoing in the space between them, this had never been going to be easy.

It had to be done, though.

He was here to hold her to her promise. She had to be his wife.

He'd wanted her even back when they'd been friends. Right from the first moment he saw her standing in the stacks in the college library, her red hair glowing in a shaft of dusty sunlight, her skin pale as porcelain, her eyes green as grass.

But an affair with her had never been on the cards. She'd been nothing but sunshine and warmth, while he'd been all darkness and doubt, and he hadn't wanted any part of his darkness to touch her. Friendship was all he could do and friends they were.

Until that night in Soho when she'd told him she loved him, and he knew he couldn't be friends with her any longer.

He'd been in shock that night, not expecting her confession. No one had ever said those words to him before, not one person, and to hear them from her...

Every part of him had wanted to take her in his arms and cover her mouth, kiss her senseless, tell her that he loved her too, that he didn't want to leave her. He never wanted to leave her.

Except his father had died and his country was in turmoil, and he'd *had* to leave. He had to take the throne he was heir to. He was responsible for protecting his people and it wasn't a duty he could walk away from.

So he'd walked away from her instead.

Love wasn't permitted for kings; he'd learned that from an early age. Emotion in general wasn't permitted. Kings had to make hard decisions, they had to do terrible things to protect people, and for him to make those decisions and do those terrible things he had to be hard too. Harder than stone.

It had been necessary to walk away from her. He couldn't be the man he'd been in England, Sidonie's friend. He couldn't be a man at all. He had to be a king. And so that was what he'd become.

He'd told her he wouldn't be coming back to England, and that she shouldn't contact him again, because he'd had to. It had been harsh, but he hadn't wanted her to live in hope he'd ever return her feelings, that he'd ever return, full stop.

It was always the sharpest cuts that healed the fastest.

He'd never thought he'd go back on that decision, either, not until the question of marriage and heirs had been brought up by his advisors. Not until he'd looked at the list of potential queens that had been suggested, and he'd seen they were all women with families who wanted position and influence in his court, perpetuating the cycle of intrigue and corruption once again.

He'd always intended to rule differently from his father, and his time in England with Sidonie had taught him about the power of laughter. Of happiness. Of hope. He wanted that for his people after the trauma of his father's reign, and, while he couldn't provide that laughter and happiness and hope himself, his queen could.

A queen like Sidonie.

He'd been toying with that idea while he'd looked over marriage contracts, which had then got him thinking about the promise Sidonie had written on that serviette. The one she'd made him sign.

It had come to him then, blindingly, that the answer had been staring him in the face all this time. The woman who'd taught him how to laugh, how to enjoy the simple pleasures in life, how to be an ordinary person, the woman who'd given him a taste of happiness... She could be his queen. She could bring all those precious qualities he'd once admired, her honesty and empathy, and warmth, to Al Da'ira. She could help him bring joy back to a country which had been crushed under the heel of a tyrant.

He'd hadn't wanted to contact her again. Taking his crown and cutting out the corruption that had been endemic in his court had turned him from mere stone into granite, and he wasn't the young man she remembered, the friend she'd once had. He'd wanted her to have only good memories of him.

But making the hard decisions was what was what being a king meant. It also meant living with the consequences so his people would have a better life. Balancing the needs of the few with the needs of the many. And the many needed Sidonie.

They needed her laughter. Her brightness. Her optimism and her empathy. Her ability to relate to people from all walks of life.

So he'd made the decision to hold her to the promise she'd written, and once he decided something, it happened. He never regretted and he never doubted. Certainty was strength in a king, another thing his mother had taught him long ago.

Sidonie would likely refuse, especially considering how he'd broken off their friendship, so he was going to have to convince her. He wouldn't accept a 'no'.

It would have been easier to do things the old way, the way of his ancestors from centuries past who simply put their chosen bride over the front of their horse and rode off with her. But, since he lived in the modern world and that was frowned upon, he'd have to go about getting her agreement instead.

Sidonie's laugh had wound down, and she was wiping her eyes, though he suspected that was for effect. 'I'm sorry, Khalil,' she said. 'For a minute there I thought you were serious.'

He did not smile. 'I am serious.'

'No, you're not.' All the laughter drained abruptly from her face. 'This is a joke.'

'You were not joking when you wrote it,' he pointed out.

'I was drunk when I wrote it.'

'You had had two Cosmopolitans and were mildly tipsy at best.'

He thought she might laugh again, one of her delightful, bubbling laughs, but she didn't. Instead her green eyes narrowed. 'You can't possibly expect to hold me to that.'

Interesting. She was…harder than he remembered. Sharper too. Not the passionate, warm woman he remembered. What had happened in the past five years to make her assume this…veneer? Because something had. Well, he'd find out. Once she was his wife, they'd have time to discuss it.

'I can,' he said flatly. 'And I will. You signed it. I'm sure I could even have my lawyers prove it is a legal contract that you are obliged to honour.' He didn't want to force the issue or hold a legal threat over her head, but the fact remained that he needed a queen. A royal marriage to give his people something joyful after all the years of his father's dark reign. And his queen had to be her.

Apart from what she herself would bring to the role, she also had no ties to his country, no family trying to gain influence, no political or business affiliations that would cause suspicion in the various factions in his court. She was an outsider with no previous history, which also made her someone most people would accept.

Sidonie's pretty features were almost hard. 'I have lawyers too, Khalil.'

He tilted his head, surveying her, noting the glitter in her eyes and the firm line of her soft mouth. Somehow she'd found steel. He wasn't sure he liked it. Where had the Sidonie he remembered gone? The Sidonie he'd been able to talk to about anything and mostly had, except for a couple of dark instances that he didn't want to remember himself, let alone talk about? The Sidonie who'd steadfastly ignored the fact that he was a prince? Who'd dragged him along to the movies and bought him popcorn. Who'd made him hold her shopping bags as if he was a servant while she tried on clothes. Who'd laughed at him when he'd told her he never carried a wallet because he always had someone to handle payments for him, and who'd then taught him how to use a debit card.

Back then he hadn't known why any of that had fascinated him so much. He'd only known she was beautiful and interesting, and that she seemed to like him. He'd never encountered that before. He'd had Augustine and Galen, of course, his friends and fellow princes, and they seemed to like him too. Yet in a way, Augustine and Galen and he had been forced together because they were all princes.

Sidonie, on the other hand, was nothing like him. She wasn't royal or rich, didn't come from nobility or money. She was friendly and warm, bright and sunny, while he'd been dark and scarred from the things he'd had to do to become heir. Despite that though, she'd seen something in him that had made her choose to be his friend.

That Sidonie would never have mentioned lawyers.

He should have paid more attention to what she'd been doing these last five years, but he'd cut off contact with her for a reason. He hadn't wanted to be distracted by the past. Not when he had the difficult politics of his nation to handle.

Not that there was any point thinking about that now.

'Then by all means engage them and we will fight this in the courts.' He held her gaze. 'I hope you have deep pockets.'

For some reason the flush that had crept through

her cheeks deepened. 'You can't mean this. Five years ago you told me not to contact you, and yet suddenly you're here, shoving some ridiculous thing I wrote when I was drunk in my face, and demanding that I marry you? That's insane, Khalil.'

It probably was from her point of view. Still, he wasn't budging.

'It is not insane,' he said. 'I am in full possession of all my faculties, I assure you. There were reasons I told you not to contact me, but things have changed.'

'What things? Changed how?'

'Al Da'ira is more stable politically now, and I need a wife.'

'But I—'

'We can discuss that later. You made me a promise, Sidonie, and you will honour it.'

'And if I don't? What? You'll take me to court?'

Each word was spiked with something serrated, falling like an icy-edged little snowflake, cold against his skin, and Khalil felt something stir deep inside him.

He stilled, a ripple of shock arrowing down his spine.

It had been years since he'd felt that part of him stir. The hunger that had helped him win his crown, the old blood that ran in his veins, a poisonous gift from his father. After his coronation he'd buried that part of himself and he'd thought it had stayed buried.

Apparently not. Apparently all you need for it to wake is a challenge.

That may be, but he was done with challenges

now. He was the King, he had nothing to prove, and certainly not where Sidonie was concerned. The cost was too high should that part of himself wake again. It had to stay frozen. It *had* to.

Khalil stared at her. He couldn't afford resistance. He needed a wife and heirs, and his people needed a queen untainted by the labyrinthine politics of his father's reign. He could go back to the list of potential candidates his advisors had put forward and choose one of them. Or, if he wanted to find a woman from outside Al Da'ira, he'd no doubt find one—he'd never had any issues with finding women who wanted him.

But he didn't want just any woman. He wanted the woman who'd taught him what happiness had felt like, because if she could do that for him, then she could do it for his people.

'Yes,' he said coolly. 'That is what I said.'

She didn't flinch, another sign of the steel she'd somehow acquired. 'So, you're going to force me to marry you. Is that what you're saying?'

She is not the same Sidonie you knew.

No. But still, it had only been five years. She could not have changed *so* much in five years.

'It will not involve force.' He kept his voice level. 'You wanted to marry me, remember? If you had not found a husband by the time you were thirty, you would marry me—that is what you said. You were very, very definite.'

'But I wasn't—'

'You wrote that promise yourself,' he went on relentlessly. 'You insisted. Because you wanted me to hold you to it when the time came.'

She opened her mouth then shut it again, her gaze flickering. The flush in her pale cheeks had crept down her lovely white throat.

She remembered that night as well as he, about how they'd been talking of him taking the throne and what it would mean for his country. He'd mentioned that he'd have to marry at some stage, and that was when she'd said that if he couldn't find someone he liked, and she was still unmarried by thirty, he could marry her.

He'd thought it was a joke at first, but there had been something intense in her eyes as she'd said it. Then she'd pulled out her cocktail serviette and had written her promise to him, signing it and getting him to sign it too.

He'd wanted to tell her that she didn't need to make him sign some ridiculous promise. He would have married her right then and there. He knew how lonely her childhood had been and how much she'd wanted a family of her own. He knew all about the awful aunt who'd brought her up and resented every second of it.

But he was the heir to the throne of Al Da'ira, not the ordinary man he'd wished so passionately he could be in that moment. And he couldn't give her that future.

He'd loved those years in England with her, but they were never going to be anything more than an idyll. A brief moment of sunshine between storms.

He had a country to rule and a crown to wear, and the king he'd been brought up to be had nothing to do with the man he'd become in England. The two were incompatible. She deserved more anyway. He wasn't capable of giving her the kind of life she needed, and he didn't want to be Hades to her Persephone, dragging her down into his Underworld.

Yet because she was his friend, and he would have given her the moon if she'd asked for it, he'd signed her serviette. And he'd never thought he'd return to make good on his promise, yet the needs of his people outweighed all other concerns.

He had to convince her somehow.

'Well, I didn't mean it,' Sidonie said now, still cool. 'So you can take that ridiculous contract and—'

'Sidonie,' he interrupted, because he was tired of sitting in this sticky, musty English pub. They could have this argument later, in cleaner, nicer surroundings, when the shock of his sudden arrival had worn off. 'You must consider my proposal. I insist. Perhaps there is something you need from me that I could give you in return?'

'I don't need anything—'

'Think on it. In the meantime,' he gestured at the cupcake, 'eat your birthday cake and then we will leave.'

There were tiny green sparks in her eyes. 'Leave? What do you mean, leave?'

Khalil was normally a patient man. The heir to the throne wasn't permitted to marry until they'd been crowned, and he'd had to wait longer than most because his father had taken his time dying. Then, after his own coronation, he'd had to tidy up the mess Amir had left. It had all taken time. Too much time. He wasn't getting any younger and the business of heirs needed to be seen to now the political situation had been handled, and he didn't want to wait any more.

He'd expected some resistance when he'd arrived, but he'd thought that she'd at least be open to discussion, and it was irritating to get a flat 'no' immediately. However, her resistance wasn't insurmountable. There were ways he could make her more receptive to him. He hadn't, for example, explored the extent of their physical chemistry yet. He'd wanted to, but he'd never crossed that line with her, and not because she didn't want him, because she had. No, he'd decided it was better not to start something he couldn't finish, and so he'd kept his distance.

If she agreed to be his wife, there was no need for that now.

'I mean,' he said calmly, 'that we will leave England and return to Al Da'ira.'

Shock rippled across her face. 'Leave England? But you can't be…'

He didn't wait for her to finish. He didn't want her thinking too hard about this or arguing further. So he leaned forward, took the balloon from her fingers and held it out wordlessly. One of his security detail sprang to take it from his hand and then did the same when he picked the cupcake up and held that out too. When they were both taken care of he rose, stepped from the booth, and held out a hand. 'Come, *ya hayati*. We can have this discussion on the way to the helicopter.'

'The helicopter?' Her self-possession wavered and she stared at him as if she'd never seen him before in her entire life. And to be fair she probably hadn't. She'd only seen the man. She'd never seen the King.

A good thing, in that case. Better she saw him as he was now rather than thinking he was still the same man he'd once been.

He wasn't her friend any longer. He couldn't afford to be.

The King was merciless, pitiless. The King protected his country with his life and so he had to be harder than the rock his palace was carved out of. Harder than iron. Hard so the enemies of his country would shatter dashing themselves against him while he remained strong, a bulwark for his people.

To them *he* was the power and the glory, to be feared and obeyed. If not, there was the possibility that the unrest that had already cost his country so much would return, and he could not permit that. Not again.

But you don't want her to fear you. Fear wasn't supposed to be part of this.

No, and it wouldn't. If he had to take the time to convince her of the rightness of this marriage, then he would have to take the time. He wasn't his father. He wasn't.

'Yes, the helicopter,' he said. 'I have another birthday surprise for you.'

Except it was clear that she didn't want any more birthday surprises, because her beautiful green eyes turned sharp as broken glass, and her delectably soft-looking mouth firmed in a way that was most un-Sidonie-like.

'No,' she said flatly. 'I am not going anywhere with you.'

CHAPTER TWO

KHALIL REGARDED HER impassively for a couple of
moments. Then, without a word, he turned on his
heel and walked out of the door.

She was still staring after him, the anger that had
been steadily building in response to his ridiculous
demand knotting inside her, when two of his security detail approached her booth. They said nothing,
merely stood to attention on either side of it, and it
took her a full minute to realise that they were waiting for her.

For a second all she could do was sit there seeth-
ing. Apparently, after presenting her with that ridiculous promise she could barely remember writing, let
alone signing, he assumed she'd follow obediently.
That she'd say yes and do whatever he wanted. Fly
off in his stupid helicopter to Al Da'ira.

Perhaps the Sidonie of five years ago, desperately
in love with a man so far out of her league he may as
well have been on Pluto, would have done so. That
Sidonie would have fallen gratefully into his arms
and let him take her anywhere.

But she wasn't that Sidonie any more. Now she was busy and her life was full. She had friends and colleagues, and Mr Sparkle, her cat. She didn't need him.

The two men standing on either side of her booth didn't move and it was clear they weren't going to leave until she did. She was very tempted to keep sitting there purely because Khalil expected her to follow him, but, since she didn't want to cause any trouble for his men—it wasn't their fault their king was an arrogant idiot—and giving Khalil a piece of her mind was far too attractive, she got to her feet and walked briskly out of the pub, the men beside the booth hurrying after her.

Outside there was quite a commotion.

The pub faced onto a large village green and sitting in the middle of the green was a sleek black helicopter. A crowd of small children was standing near by gazing in awe at it, and Sidonie found herself staring as Khalil strode straight over to them. He smiled and crouched down, digging into his pockets as he did so and bringing something out, handing whatever it was to the awestruck children. Then he said something and they all scattered like a flock of seagulls, whooping and shouting as they did so. All the while the black-clad security men gently ushered a few gawking adults away from the helicopter as the rotors began to spin.

She came to a stop, staring at him, watching the hard, sharp lines of his face soften as he spoke with the children. And, despite everything she'd told herself, her heart twisted behind her ribs. Just for a moment he'd looked like Khal, the man who'd once been her best friend. The man whose smiles had lit up her world and whose deep, soft laugh had made even the depths of winter feel like summer.

But as the children scattered the warmth left his expression and his features hardened. He rose to his full height and strode over to the helicopter. There, he finally paused and glanced in her direction, and she felt one of the security guys grab her elbow. Then, much to her shock, she found herself being ushered firmly towards the helicopter.

'Wait,' she said breathlessly, more startled than anything else. 'I said I didn't want to—'

But everything got lost beneath the noise of the rotors and then she momentarily lost the power of speech as the man holding her handed her over to Khalil, whose strong fingers closed around her elbow. Even through the light cotton of her shirt she could feel the warmth of his skin, his grip firm and assured, sending shivers through her.

It had been years since she'd been this close to him, years since he'd touched her, and she found herself unable to pull away as he guided her into the sleek machine with effortless strength, sitting her down in a seat of soft black leather. A headset was put on her and her seatbelt buckled. Then the door was being closed and he was beside her, speaking to the pilot in Arabic, then the whole thing shuddered before lifting off into the air.

What are you doing? You weren't supposed to be going anywhere with him, remember?

She stared at the seat in front of her, trying to get some oxygen into her suddenly starving lungs, and her brain, which had somehow disengaged the moment he'd taken her elbow, into gear again.

What was wrong with her? She *hadn't* wanted to go with him. What she'd been going to do was give him a piece of her mind then go to find Derek and continue with the date, not follow Khalil obediently. Yet…the moment he'd grasped her elbow she'd been like a kitten taken by the scruff of the neck, relaxing into his grip as if there was nowhere else she'd wanted to be.

And now it was too late to get away from him. They were in the air.

A bolt of something that wasn't quite fear shot through her, and not because she was afraid of where he was taking her, or even of him. No, she was afraid of what being close to him after all this time might do to her.

You can't let him hurt you…not again.

No, she couldn't. That email he'd sent her, cutting her off and dismissing their friendship as if it had never been, had devastated her, reminding her of the day she'd lost her parents with the sheer abruptness of it.

Of course, she knew why he'd sent it. She'd ruined their friendship by telling him she loved him. Her own fault, naturally. She'd always been too emotionally demanding, as her aunt had always said.

Except she'd thought he was different. He'd never made her feel emotionally needy or too demanding. Even when she'd forgotten herself at times and got angry with him, he'd simply let her say her piece and then discuss it with her. He'd never told her she was being ridiculous or threatened her with being left at an orphanage the way her aunt had.

Apparently, though, he hadn't been different that night, and now he was back as if he hadn't broken her heart, telling her things had changed, and he wanted to marry her, and she was just expected to accept it?

Was he actually out of his mind?

Anger simmered inside her once again, edging out that not-quite-fear, but she tried to ignore it. She didn't want him to know that he'd hurt her, because she didn't want him still to matter.

He does matter, though. You can't deny it. You wouldn't be so angry otherwise.

No. Her anger was just a reflex because she didn't like being ordered around. Once, he'd mattered to her more than anyone or anything in the entire world, but not now. She might still be attracted to him admittedly, but nothing more.

'I thought I said I *didn't* want to go anywhere with you,' she said coolly.

'You did say that.' His voice was calm, his posture relaxed as he leaned back in his seat. 'Yet you seemed to have no problem getting into the helicopter.'

The sun was going down, long streams of fading light glossing his black hair. She was conscious of his nearness, one powerful thigh almost touching hers, and she could smell his warm, spicy, familiar scent. Sandalwood and cloves, and the musky, masculine scent that was all his own.

He was so very beautiful…

She couldn't stop yet another shiver. No matter what she told herself about how he didn't matter any more, she was still as mesmerised by him now as she had been the first moment in the library when she'd heard that deep, dark voice of his behind her, asking a question. And she'd turned around to answer it…

As if he knew exactly what she was thinking, his hard mouth curved.

He looked exceptionally pleased with himself.

'Smugness doesn't suit you, Khalil,' she said, ignoring her simmering anger. 'Didn't you listen to me when I said no?'

He raised one winged brow. 'Were you forced at gunpoint? I do not think so.'

Well, even five years ago he hadn't been quite *this* confident.

Being a king did not suit him either, she decided.

'You should have asked me if I wanted to come,' she said. 'And you didn't.'

'You could have walked away at any time.' His gaze settled on her. 'And you didn't.'

She wanted to tell him he was wrong, that of course she could have walked away, but the words suddenly felt slippery and hard to grasp. Her whole world seemed to be consumed by that look in his eyes. It was so familiar, as if she was the only thing worth looking at in the entire universe. God, how she'd loved that. Loved it with her whole heart.

Those five years she'd spent as his friend had been the happiest of her life. She'd become someone new when she met him, someone brighter and more vivid, someone interesting, someone…extraordinary.

And you remember how it was when he left.

Oh, she did. It had felt as if she'd lost part of her soul. As if he'd taken all her passion and joy and optimism with him when he'd left, leaving her with only the worst parts of herself. The fear and the anger and the grief.

She'd been in a dark place after that, and it had only been sheer determination and the needs of her charity that had stopped her from succumbing to the pain and falling into the darkness. She wasn't going back there, not ever.

Turning away would be an admission of weakness, but she couldn't stand the intensity in his eyes, or the gravitational force of his physical charisma, so she glanced out of the window at the landscape unrolling beneath them instead, pretending it was an idle look, nothing more.

'You should have talked to me first.' She smoothed the fine black wool of her trousers.

'I did talk to you first.'

'That was not a discussion.'

There was no response, and she couldn't help glancing back, only to find that his dark, disturbing gaze hadn't moved. 'Do not be afraid, *ya hayati,*' he said, his voice softer and quieter. 'You know I will not hurt you.'

Too late for that, she wanted to say. But she didn't.

She smoothed the fabric of her trousers yet again, trying to find her equilibrium. 'Purely out of interest, why are you so set on marrying me? You must have more suitable candidates surely?'

Again, he was silent, his gaze just as enigmatic as it had been seconds earlier. 'I think now is not the time for that conversation. We will talk more about that when we get there.'

Briefly Sidonie considered arguing, but he'd always been a stubborn man and she suspected he'd be absolutely impossible now. Besides, getting emotional never helped anything—she'd learned that all too well. Her aunt had hated any what she termed 'fusses'. Best to keep her head as she had the moment he'd walked into the pub.

'And where is there?' she enquired. 'Surely we're not flying all the way to Al Da'ira in your helicopter?'

The intensity had died out of his eyes and he was now regarding her with a certain detached amusement. 'No. I have changed my mind. I am taking you out to dinner instead.'

Surprise rippled through her. 'Dinner?'

'We have not seen each other for some time and you have doubts. Therefore we need to talk and I did not want to talk in that pub. There are more pleasant places to discuss our marriage, so it is to one of them that we are going. Also, it is your birthday.'

'Our' marriage, he'd said. As if it was already a foregone conclusion. As if she had no say in this whatsoever. It reminded her of the day her parents had died, after her aunt had collected her from school, told her the awful news, and had brought her back home, even though it wasn't her home any longer. May had instructed her to collect her things, because Sidonie would be coming to live with her. The look on her aunt's face as she'd said it had been pure resignation, and Sidonie had known then and there that her aunt hadn't wanted to be saddled with her. But, since May had been her only living relative, neither of them had had a choice.

'Keep carrying on like that and I'll drop you at the nearest orphanage,' May had told her once, when Sidonie had had a tantrum about something small. 'The only reason you're here at all is because I had a duty to your father. But don't think I can't change my mind.'

Sidonie had never thought that. In fact, she'd lived in fear of it, making sure she wasn't demanding or bothersome. Being careful not to cause any 'fuss'. She toed the line, giving her aunt no reason to complain.

It had been hard, but then again, she'd been a child and hadn't had a choice about any of it. It was either her aunt or a foster home and she hadn't wanted that either.

The memory made anger gather into a tight, hot ball, shot through with jagged edges of hurt, but she calmly folded her hands over it, keeping it inside. 'And where is dinner?'

This time his smile touched his dark eyes briefly, a flash of his old warmth, and her heart gave a little quiver in her chest. 'I thought we'd have dinner in Paris.'

For the second time in an hour, Sidonie found herself blinking at him. Paris? He was taking her to Paris?

She fought to find her voice. 'In that case it's a pity I don't have my passport.'

'You do,' he said. 'I had my staff retrieve it. Your cat will also be taken care of.'

That hot ball squeezed tight inside her. 'But I have work—'

'I will contact your supervisor and inform them that you will not be there tomorrow,' Khalil interrupted smoothly. 'Do not worry.'

Shock at the sheer gall of the man stole her breath. He'd somehow found out where she lived and got her passport, had her cat taken care of, and now he thought he could ring her 'supervisor' and tell them she wouldn't be there. As if she were nothing more than a chess piece he could move around whenever he liked, with no thought to her feelings.

Something prickled at the backs of her eyes, but it surely couldn't be tears. She didn't cry about anything these days. It didn't matter that he was treating her as if she was a stranger he didn't particularly care about. Because she didn't care either.

She didn't care about him.

'I'm sure you didn't used to be this arrogant,' she said. 'What happened?'

His gaze glittered in the setting sun. 'I became a king, Sidonie.'

A creeping sense of dislocation hit her in that moment. He looked the same as she remembered, his face with all those beautifully carved planes and angles so familiar to her. The face of her once best friend. Yet there was a hardness to his strong jaw, a firmness to his mouth, a sharp intensity in his eyes.

He *was* a king. And it had changed him.

You aren't the same and neither is he.

That was true. She'd changed in the past five years, and she couldn't expect him to have stayed the same. Especially not since he'd been on the throne. The friend she remembered, who'd been puzzled by the existence of debit cards and then had been delighted when she'd shown him to use one, who'd been arrogant and yet had waited patiently outside a department-store changing room holding five shopping bags so she could try on clothes, who'd been intense and passionate about wanting to make the lives of his people better, encouraging her in her own dreams of starting a charity, had gone.

The man at her side looked iron-hard, and there was no passion at all in his dark, cold eyes. A stranger's eyes.

Perhaps she needed to start thinking of him like that now. As a stranger. It would certainly mean less hurt for her as well as helping her to keep her distance.

Khalil raised a brow. 'Lost for words? Surely not.'

She swallowed, her mouth suddenly dry. If she was going to think of him as a stranger then here she was, in a helicopter, being taken to Paris, essentially kidnapped by a man she didn't know. A man who was a king, who apparently had taken it into his head to marry her.

He wouldn't hurt her—not physically at least—and she wasn't afraid of him in that way. But she was afraid of being swept away from the life she'd built for herself. A successful life with important work and people who depended on and needed her. She didn't want to leave it. She couldn't leave it.

You will have to resist him.

The words whispered through her head, and she took a quick, silent breath, conscious of his intense stare. He was so very beautiful.

But no, resisting him was easy. All she had to do was think of how much it had hurt when he'd walked away and how she never wanted to open herself up to that level of pain again.

There. Easy.

'Not lost for words. I'm just considering what to say next, because you do understand that I have no supervisor, don't you?'

His expression remained impassive, but she thought she saw a flicker of surprise in his eyes, which sent an odd little ripple of satisfaction through her.

What had he thought she'd been doing these last five years? That she'd just be sitting around on her hands mourning him?

'Are you working for yourself, then?' he asked, the surprise gone as if it had never been.

'You must have forgotten the charity I started up,' she said acidly. 'Remember? We talked about it a few months before you left.'

'Yes,' he said expressionlessly. 'I remember.'

'Well, it's grown a lot since then and I have many people depending on me. If I'm not going to be back in London before tomorrow, I will need to make some calls.'

'I see.' The words sounded very neutral and yet she knew they were not. There were undertones in his voice, a thread of yet more surprise perhaps, or annoyance—she didn't know which.

The satisfaction that she'd knocked his seemingly unassailable confidence deepened. 'You didn't know, did you?' This time it was her turn to raise a brow. 'Perhaps you should have investigated that before you came back. Contrary to what you might think, I actually have a life of my own and it's a very successful one, thank you very much.'

Khalil's expression remained as impassive as ever. 'Clearly,' he said.

'In fact,' she went on, since she might as well, 'I bet there are many other things you don't know about me, Khalil.' She paused. 'Or should that be Your Majesty?'

Sparks glittered in his eyes just then, and she wasn't sure if it was the last rays of the setting sun catching them or something else, but it suddenly felt as if all the remaining air in the helicopter had been sucked out of it.

His gaze roamed over her face, studying her as if he'd never seen her before in his life, and she was once again suddenly and painfully aware of him. Of the lithe strength of his body and the pull of his trousers across his powerful thighs. Of his warmth. Of the bronze skin of his throat and the pulse that beat there, strong and steady.

The night of her birthday he'd pulled her into his arms for a dance. She'd never been that close to him before. She'd never been that close to any man before, let alone one so tall. He'd felt hard and hot, and her heart had been beating so fast. She hadn't known what it was she was feeling, at first. Then she'd understood...

Her heart was beating that fast now; she could hear it resounding in her head.

That hint of a smile curved one corner of his mouth again, as if he'd seen something that pleased him. 'I appreciate "Your Majesty",' he said, his voice almost on the edge of a purr. '"Sir" is also acceptable. My people, of course, call me a god, but that would be a step too far for you, I think.'

Sidonie's mouth had become even drier. She didn't need that memory in her head, not when it felt as if there was a fine current of electricity in the air around them, making her skin prickle and tighten.

He'd never looked at her this way before, with heat. He'd never given even the slightest hint that he was interested in her in that way. Yet that electricity was unmistakable, as was the look in his eyes...

She glanced away, flustered and hating herself for being flustered. She'd had very little experience with men. As a teenager she'd spent too much time trying to get good marks at school to allow time for crushes, and then, at Oxford, she'd met Khalil, and of course no other man would ever or could ever measure up to him. After he'd left England, and she'd decided she was going to put him behind her once and for all, she'd tried the dating scene. But was soon faced with the hard, cold reality that the men she'd met didn't interest her. So after a year or two of disappointment, Sidonie had decided she didn't want anything to do with them full stop.

Except now, sitting next to Khalil and not knowing what to say because of the way he was looking at her, to not even be able to hold his gaze... She was regretting that decision. It was ridiculous to be thirty and still a virgin, to be so inexperienced that her ex-best friend could fluster her with a mere look.

It gave him too much power and he was already far too powerful as it was.

So? Take some of it back.

Yes, but how? She would have to think more about it.

Sidonie looked down at her white shirt and brushed at an imaginary speck of lint to cover her fluster. 'They call you a god? Do people still believe the King is semi-divine, then? Surely not after your father.'

He shrugged. 'They decided he was too flawed to be divine. He was merely a man and should not be venerated.'

Sidonie knew about his country, because he'd talked about it. It was fantastically rich due to its oil deposits and also had a very Byzantine political system where the King or Queen's word was absolute law, bolstered by the belief that, since an ordinary human being could never protect a nation, the ruler should be a god.

It had always sounded like a very interesting place, and she'd have loved to visit, but he'd warned her off travelling there. He hadn't wanted to show her Al Da'ira under his father's rule, because Amir had turned it into such a hotbed of corruption and nepotism. 'Come when I am King,' Khalil had said. 'I will show you the true heart of Al Da'ira then.'

She still remembered those conversations. About all the things Khalil would change when he was King. His passion had been so inspiring. But...where had that man gone?

He's a stranger, remember? You can't think of him as your friend any more.

'Then should I be prostrating myself in your presence?' She kept her voice light and casual. 'Make sure my face is pressed to the floor?'

'No need to prostrate yourself. Kneeling in my presence would be fine.' In the depths of his eyes, that ember of heat sparked again, and there was a wicked edge to that slight smile.

It shocked her, that heat. As did the sensual note in

his voice. It was as if they were talking about something completely to different from what they were actually talking about.

Don't be stupid. He's flirting with you.

Sidonie took another breath, that sense of dislocation hitting her again, making her almost dizzy. Of course that was what he was doing. And it was strange because he'd never flirted with her before. He was arrogant, yes, but he could also be charming when he wanted to be, and she'd watched him make slaves of people with only one of his rare smiles. But he'd never turned that charm on her. She'd been pleased that he didn't, telling herself that it was because she didn't need charming. She was his friend, not a girlfriend. Except a secret part of her had always longed for him to flirt with her, look at her the way he was doing now, with heat.

Don't fall for him again. You can't afford to.

Shoving away the silly, quivering part of her, she met his gaze coolly. 'No one is kneeling, Khalil. Least of all me.'

If he found her lack of flirtatious response annoying, he gave no sign. 'Never say never, Sidonie,' he said, his voice giving nothing away. 'You should enjoy the view before the sun sets. We will talk more on this later.'

She didn't protest this time, and when he pulled his phone from his pocket and glanced down at it, indicating that he was done talking, she only felt relief. She needed a break to think about how she was going to handle this supposed dinner.

The rest of the short flight, Sidonie tried to pay attention to the view from the window, but her thoughts kept circling around this dinner they were going to have when they finally arrived, and what she was going to say to him if he kept on insisting that she marry him.

He'd mentioned something back in the pub in England, asking her to think about whether there was something she might need from him, but the only thing she could possibly need from him was his continued distance.

What about for the charity? He's a king. He could be useful.

Sidonie scowled out of the window. Unfortunately, yes, in that way he could be useful. She'd been looking for a patron to help boost the charity's profile, and having a royal one would be even better than the celebrities she'd been considering approaching.

He could give the charity a global reach, even beyond Europe if he agreed. And all for the small price of marrying him.

But think of how many children you could help.

It was true. And helping orphaned and disadvantaged children had been the whole reason she'd started it, having once been one of those children herself.

She thought about it the rest of the flight, until Paris was suddenly laid out beneath her, the Eiffel Tower in the distance, and then it vanished from her head.

She'd been to France once, on a school trip years

ago, and all she could remember was that it had been cold and everyone had complained. But now it was here, glittering in the darkness as the helicopter swooped over the city before coming in to land on a large expanse of green lawn that appeared to be part of a private residence.

Despite herself, an excited little thrill shot through her.

Apart from that one school trip, she'd never been abroad, and certainly she hadn't while she'd been working on building up the charity. She'd been too busy to think of taking a holiday let alone where to take one. But if she'd had time, Paris would certainly have been top of her list. All those ancient churches and delicious food and rich history and culture...

You talked about it with him once, remember?

Another memory drifted through her head, of one night in her college rooms, where he'd joined her to study, and they'd talked about travel and the other places he'd been to, which had then evolved into a discussion about all the places she wanted to go, including Paris. Had he remembered that? Was that why they were here?

Again, if he'd done it five years earlier, she would have been thrilled. She was less so now, especially when he hadn't even asked if she wanted to go. Now, with his sudden reappearance in her life and this marriage demand, it felt...calculated almost.

The thought sat uncomfortably in her head as the helicopter door was pulled open and Khalil got out. He handed both his headset and Sidonie's to an aide, but when another aide approached he gave him a sharp look. The man bowed his head and dropped back as Khalil turned to her, holding out his arm.

'Come,' he said regally. 'I will escort you myself.'

There were people watching her and, since she didn't want to create a drama by protesting, she laid her fingers on his forearm, feeling warm wool and hard muscle, the power that he held contained within that magnificent body of his. It was rock-solid, that arm, and she had the sense, as she climbed awkwardly out of the machine, that she could lean her whole weight on it and it wouldn't move.

But she didn't want to think about how good he felt, so she forced the feeling away as he led her through an ornate and magnificent garden, towards an equally ornate and magnificent mansion, with stone balconies and huge windows. They went up some steps, stepping through the door into a grand hallway with a sweeping staircase and high ceilings. There were paintings on those ceilings, and glittering chandeliers hanging from them.

Khalil didn't pause as a whole army of servants surrounded them, merely continuing on straight through them as if they weren't there, guiding her up that sweeping staircase and down a long hallway. At the end of the hallway were some doors standing open onto a stone terrace.

The Eiffel Tower was squarely in front of them, taking up the whole sky, while on the terrace stood tubs of flowers and shrubs and small trees. There were candles everywhere. A small table covered with a white tablecloth stood in the middle of the terrace, and it had been set with silver cutlery and crystal glasses. In an ice bucket a bottle of champagne rested.

It was beautiful and achingly romantic. The perfect setting for an engagement.

If she'd been the old Sidonie, her heart would have burst from happiness. If she'd been the old Sidonie she would have said yes the moment he'd walked through the door.

But she wasn't the old Sidonie.

She was harder, more guarded, and that heart of hers had been broken.

He was the one who had broken it. And, while she was long over that now, she wasn't going to risk him breaking it again. Which was why her answer was always going to be 'no'.

CHAPTER THREE

KHALIL WATCHED SIDONIE'S beautiful green eyes widen, and he allowed himself a small measure of satisfaction at the flicker of awe on her face. But then, almost in the same moment, the awe was gone, her expression smoothing into that same cool mask he'd observed in the helicopter.

It annoyed him and at the same time intrigued him, he couldn't deny it. Sidonie had once been so open, never hiding anything from him. He'd always been able to tell what she was feeling and that was part of the reason he wanted her as his queen.

After the kind of childhood he'd had, brought up in his mother's house in the mountains and subject to the rigorous discipline that his mother had believed would turn him into a strong king, Sidonie's emotional honesty had seemed shocking to him at first. She'd seemed to be a relatively quiet and subdued person when they'd met, but he'd soon realised that her quietness had hidden a deeply passionate nature. She felt things deeply, the way he did, but they'd both been taught certain things about emotions, and it had taken some time to overcome those lessons and to trust each other.

Her aunt had taught her that her feelings were too demanding and needed to be controlled, while his mother had taught him that emotions were weaknesses, flaws to be exploited.

Gradually, as they'd become more open with each other, Sidonie had blossomed. She was so honest about her feelings with him, and he'd learned that there was nothing manipulative or fake about her. She always said what she meant, and he could always trust what she said.

Which was why that night in Soho, when she'd told him she loved him, had been so very hard. Because he'd known it was true. She *did* love him. She loved him and he was going to have to hurt her.

Perhaps that was why she was more guarded than she once had been, hiding behind that cool veneer of hers.

She was protecting herself because of him.

Regret twisted inside him, but he ignored it. Regret wasn't for kings. They made the decisions they did for the good of their country and they did not look back on them.

He studied her now, standing on the terrace in her tailored black trousers and plain white shirt, her red hair sleek in its little bun. Her lovely face betrayed nothing, her green eyes cool. So very self-possessed.

It made him want to know what she'd been doing these past five years. Certainly he'd made assumptions—her having a supervisor for example—that were clearly wrong, which was his own fault. He should have investigated how her charity was doing before he'd made the trip to England, but he hadn't because he'd thought... Well. He'd thought she'd still be the same as the woman he remembered. And she wasn't.

This little terrace scene he'd had his staff put together had been based on a conversation he'd had with her about Paris once, and he'd hoped it would sway her into agreeing to be his queen.

But maybe it wouldn't. Maybe she didn't care for Paris these days.

Sidonie's cool gaze met his. 'So, is this all for my benefit?'

'Yes.' There was no reason to deny it. 'Happy birthday, *ya hayati*.'

'If you think a nicely set table and an endearment will make me more likely to agree to marry you, you need to think again, Khalil.'

That poisonous part of him stirred yet again, responding to the challenge. And it *was* a challenge, whether she realised it or not. He forced it down. That part of himself could never be let out. It had to stay locked away. Not ever fully excised, because the day might come when his country needed it, and if that day came he'd have to embrace it.

Just as he'd had to embrace the battle of succession to determine his suitability to be heir. The battle was a ritualistic fight between the oldest children of each of the King's wives for the right to be the heir to the throne, a historical leftover from another time.

Khalil hadn't wanted to take part; he'd thought it medieval and outdated, but his mother had told him he couldn't afford not to.

'*You have responsibilities, Khalil,*' she'd said coldly when he'd voiced his reluctance. '*If you do not fight, then Yusuf will be named heir, and you know what he would do to this country should he become King. Protecting Al Da'ira is all that is important. What you want doesn't matter.*'

What he'd wanted never mattered. His father's blood ran too strong his veins, she'd told him, which made him more susceptible to the flaws of selfishness and vice than other people. He had to guard himself more strongly against them, never indulge his own needs. He had to learn how to place the greater good above them.

Well, he'd learned. He might have that old blood, but he didn't let it rule him. He couldn't. Not when the foundation of his kingship was *not* following in his father's footsteps.

'So, what would make you marry me?' he asked idly, since, although he had no intention of letting her walk away, everything would go much more smoothly if she wasn't actively fighting him.

'Nothing.' Her gaze was sharp. 'I don't want to marry anyone.' Before he could reply, she turned and moved across the terrace to stand at the stone parapet, her attention on the iconic shape of the Eiffel Tower in front of them. She was holding herself very stiffly, her back straight and her shoulders tense.

He studied her yet again, trying to puzzle out

what she was thinking and what had happened to
the woman he'd left behind five years earlier. Was
she still there, hiding behind this woman's cool,
smooth veneer?

He'd lost his ability to read her, that was the problem. Or rather, he'd never had to read her, because
the Sidonie he remembered had always been open
with him. But not this Sidonie. She was far more
guarded. Though, judging from her rigid posture,
he'd say she was still angry.

That was obvious.

Yes, well, he would have to get her *not* to be
angry with him, and that was going to be tricky. If
he wanted her agreement to be his queen, he would
have to find a way, which meant some convincing
was in order.

Khalil studied the stiff line of her back for a moment, then stalked over to the ice bucket and picked
up the champagne bottle. He popped the cork, poured
some of the fizzy liquid into two flutes, and carried
both over to where she stood.

'For you,' he said, holding out the glass.

She glanced at him, her expression still guarded.
She smelled of apples and cinnamon, and another
sweet scent he couldn't quite put his finger on, and
it came almost as a shock that the scent was as familiar to him as his own name, despite the years. She'd
changed, it was true, but she still smelled the same.

Desire stirred inside him, bright and sharp, which
was another shock, since he'd thought he'd put that
desire behind him.

Apparently not.

When he'd come to Oxford and become friends with Galen of Kalithera and Augustine of Isavere, his companion 'Wicked Princes' and two men who knew the unique demands of being an heir to the throne, they'd turned the university town upside down. There had been parties and wildness, and all kinds of beautiful women, and he'd indulged himself completely, using them to forget the terrible price he'd paid to be the heir, not to mention the doubt and the guilt that had followed him to England.

Yet no other woman had ever captured the unique combination of curvaceousness, sensuality and warmth that was Sidonie.

If he hadn't been a prince, if he'd been an ordinary student, he'd have seduced her in minutes back then. But the life of an ordinary student had never been his destiny. He'd been intended for the isolation of command, the cold logic of difficult decisions and heavy scales to balance. A man in control of a country couldn't be the same man who laughed in a pub or screamed at a football match or held a grieving friend on the anniversary of her parents' death.

Friendship was all he had to give and so he'd never crossed that line.

Yet for some reason now, standing close to her, with the achingly familiar scent of her winding around him, reminding him of things he'd purposefully forgotten, all those reasons seemed pointless now.

If she agreed, she would be his wife and heirs

would need to be conceived. He could have her naked beneath him, and then he could put his mouth to her throat, finally taste her skin the way he'd always fantasised about, breathe in that delicious scent...

His body hardened and yet again he was conscious of deep surprise. Nothing happened unless he willed it, especially when it came to physical reactions, and for baser parts of himself to react to her without his control...

He realised she was studying him, so he ignored the grip of desire and met her gaze. 'Take the glass, Sidonie. I will not hold it for ever.'

She took the glass, and he observed that she didn't let her fingers brush his.

He raised his own glass. 'A toast,' he said. 'To your birthday.'

She looked at him a moment longer, then raised hers too, taking a small sip. 'So,' she said. 'What were you doing with those children in the village? You gave them something.'

Interesting that she should have noticed that.

'I gave them some money.' He took a sip of his own champagne. 'And then told them that the first person to find four totally round and smooth rocks and bring them to one of my men would receive another ten pounds.'

Her brow creased. 'Why?'

Did she think he wouldn't have thought about or noticed the attention his chopper had drawn when he'd landed it in the middle of the village green? Of course he had. Then again, she'd always thought he was too arrogant for his own good and she wasn't wrong. But kings had to be arrogant. Without confidence in themselves and their decisions, how could their people trust them? And without trust, how could they rule effectively? Confidence and certainty were strengths, and he was nothing if not strong.

His mother had made sure of that. Her methods had been...unorthodox, but he'd survived them. And his reign would be the better for them.

'I wanted to get them away from the helicopter, since we were about to take off.' He swirled the liquid in his glass. 'Also, I like children.'

The cool expression on her face rippled, betraying surprise. 'You do?'

Had she forgotten their discussions? About their dreams for the future? He'd never made any secret of the fact that he wanted to have a family one day. He had to. It was expected of him to secure the succession. Not that he'd ever have more than one wife, unlike his father. It was his father's greed that had caused all the problems after all, and outlawing polygamy had been one of Khalil's first acts as King.

'Yes,' he said. 'Do you not remember? I wanted a big family, as you did yourself. That is why you made me sign that piece of paper, after all.'

'I thought I made it clear—'

'I mean to marry you, Sidonie.' He let the steel of the King thread through his voice, so she would understand how serious he was. 'And I want it to be a marriage in every sense of the word.'

She said nothing. Then carefully put the champagne glass down on the stone of the parapet and turned to give him her full attention. 'Why?' she asked bluntly. 'It's been years since we've seen each other and even before you left you never displayed the slightest interest in me. Something's changed. What is it?'

He could only give her the truth. She expected—and deserved—nothing less. And he suspected that if he wanted her agreement, being honest with her was the only way to secure it.

'What changed?' he said after a moment. 'I became King. And I need a queen.'

'That's it? You need a queen and I randomly fit the bill somehow?'

'You are not random, Sidonie. I need a woman I can trust, and my people a queen they can look up to.'

She frowned. 'What do you mean, a queen they can look up to?'

'You know about my father's reign. You know what it did to my people.' They'd talked about it many times, all those long nights studying either in her rooms or in his. Drinking endless cups of coffee as he'd told her about his country and what his father had done to it. How his great-grandfather had reinstated polygamy so for decades the Kings of Al Da'ira had more than one wife, much to the disapproval of the rest of the world, including the neighbouring desert nations. His father had had four, and, like his father before him, had decreed that his children should battle for the crown as they had in centuries past. And so Khalil had grown up the only child of wife number three, and he'd had to fight his oldest half-sibling for the right to rule, the only one who'd been of the right age, and that had been Yusuf.

It had been a medieval childhood. A medieval and dangerous existence.

Sidonie had been shocked when he'd told her about that and the endless intrigues, assassination attempts, and corruption that his father actively encouraged. She'd asked him lots of questions and then they'd discussed how he'd bring change to his country, because they'd both agreed emphatically that change had to come.

And it had. He'd had to use force to quell the stubborn pockets of resistance who'd supported Yusuf, the sheer power of his will to lay down new laws. People had said he was too much like his father, that he was not divine, that he was only a man, and they couldn't follow a mere man.

But he'd shown them. He'd proved he wasn't his father, that he wasn't a mere man. He'd shown them that he was a king, and so they believed.

But now was not the time for more pressure. It was the time for peace and for that he needed her.

'Yes,' she said slowly. 'I remember. And you wanted to be different.'

'I have been different. But change was not easy, and my people have been…scarred.'

A look of concern flickered over her face, a glimpse of the empathic friend he remembered. 'Oh, I didn't know that. I'm sorry, Khalil. That must have been awful.'

Something inside him ached suddenly, a ghost of the longing he'd once felt for her, but he ignored it. He'd cut that feeling out of him long ago.

'It was,' he agreed. 'My people need some joy in their lives. They need hope and laughter. They need kindness and care.' He met her gaze. 'They do not need a king. What they need is a queen. What they need is you.'

Again, that cool veneer of hers rippled, betraying shock. 'Me? Why me?'

'Because you are all of those things, *ya hayati*. You are kind and compassionate. You are empathic and honest. You understand the value of laughter. In other words, you are exactly what my people need in a queen.'

Her green eyes were dark in the soft glow of the lights around them and she'd gone pale. She was looking at him as if he'd hurt her in some fashion. Then abruptly the expression vanished and she turned away, glancing at the Eiffel Tower once more.

Uncharacteristic impatience gathered inside him. He had no idea why she'd looked hurt, but had the appeal on behalf of his people not been enough?

'You taught me all of those things, Sidonie.' He tried to keep the impatience from his voice. 'You taught me what it was to have a friend and to be a friend in return. You taught me what it meant to be happy. Do you not understand? If you did that for me, you could do that for my people, too.'

Another moment or two passed and she didn't move. Then slowly she looked back at him and her gaze was just as sharp as it had been across the table in that pub in England. 'This dinner is a nice gesture and I appreciate it. But there are many other women who have all the qualities you just listed. You don't need me in particular.'

'But I—'

'I too have people who depend on me,' she interrupted steadily. 'People who need me. And I can't just leave them because you decided I'm your perfect queen.'

'Sidonie—'

'No, Khalil.' There was steel in her green eyes now. 'I'm sorry. I'm not marrying you and that's final.'

Sidonie held herself very straight and made sure her voice was very firm. She didn't care if she interrupted him, even though from the way his dark eyes flared he'd obviously considered it rude. But that was too bad. If she let him take charge again, he'd bulldoze his way over all her objections the way he had back in the pub, and she'd find herself hauled off to Al Da'ira before she knew what was happening.

She couldn't allow that.

He'd been intense about changing his people's lives for the better back then, and she could see the same intensity now in the hard planes and angles of his face. In his eyes. And it had made her waver.

This mattered to him. This mattered to him very much.

But she couldn't say yes to him. She couldn't give

up the life she'd built for herself and all the people who depended on her, all the children who needed the help her charity could give them, just because Khalil had commanded her to marry him.

Who says you need to give up all of that?

No, she didn't need that thought in her head. There would be no marriage and that was final. Because even apart from the charity and everything she'd built, she couldn't allow him back into her life, not again. Not when he'd left such devastation behind him the last time.

Khalil stood there so very tall and broad, the lights of the city falling on his compelling face. His gaze was fixed on hers, intensely focused, as if he was trying to see inside her head.

He was so close—too close. The scent of his aftershave and the warmth of his body were doing things to her that she didn't like, making her want things she shouldn't. Things she thought she'd put behind her.

She should move away, but with that gaze of his on her, seeing everything, he'd notice and he'd know the reason. She didn't want to give away how his nearness affected her, so she stayed where she was.

'No?' His voice had deepened, become rougher. 'That is really your answer? I told you it was for my people's sake.'

'I realise that.' She tried to sound calm. She didn't want to give away the real reason, not given what that would reveal about her own feelings. 'But I don't know your people. And I don't know your country.

And I…' She paused. 'It's been years, Khalil. I feel like I barely know you.'

'You do know me.'

'Do I? I knew my friend. I knew him very well, but you aren't him, are you?'

He hesitated a moment then shook his head. 'No. Not any more.'

Something she didn't understand glittered in his obsidian gaze just then, a hard edge that she was sure hadn't been there all those years ago. The hard edge she'd seen at the pub and in the helicopter.

Being King has taken its toll.

There was a strange tightness in her chest, because it was obvious now that yes, it had taken something from him. It had hardened him. Darkened him. He'd always had a darkness to him, even back at university, and she'd thought that maybe he still had some secrets he hadn't told her. Yet she hadn't pushed. If he'd wanted to tell her he would have, and she'd respected his choices.

But now…what had happened to her friend?

'Khalil,' she began, to say what she didn't know. But then he moved, putting his glass down on the parapet and taking a step closer to her. He raised a hand, and before she could draw breath he'd lifted it, cupping her cheek in one large, warm palm.

'But I still remember that man, Sidonie.' He looked down into her face, his expression fierce. 'I am not him now, but I still have his memories. He was your friend once and you were his. So, if you will not do it for my people, will you do it for him? For the sake of the friendship you once shared with him?'

She couldn't move. All the breath had left her body. Something inside her was trembling and no matter how hard she tried to ignore it, she couldn't. His fingertips lightly pressing against the side of her face burned like fire, and there was a familiar ache tightening inside her, right down between her thighs.

The glowing ember she'd seen in his eyes in that moment in the helicopter was back, lighting the darkness, turning his intensity into a force of nature that robbed her of all thought. He'd never turned it on her before, not like this…

She wanted desperately to tell him that man had also walked away from her and hurt her, to turn away so he wasn't touching her, but she couldn't bring herself to do it. It was as if she'd been waiting all her life for him to touch her like this, to cup her cheek in just this way and look down into her eyes as he was doing right now…

'I can make it worth your while, *ya hayati*.' His gaze searched her face, searing her as surely as the touch of his fingers. 'I know you still want me. I have seen it in your eyes.'

The humiliation she remembered from all those years ago crept through her. The words she'd said to him on the snowy street in Soho, and how his expression had closed up completely. How he'd turned away without a word and left her standing there alone.

That had been her last memory of him, watching him walk away while her heart had crumbled.

Her muscles tightened at the memory, but he gripped her a little harder, and murmured, 'No, Sidonie. Stay.'

'Why should I?' The words came out shaky and raw. 'You don't feel that way about me. I know you don't.'

'Do I not?' The glitter in his eyes became more intense and that was the only warning she got. The next second, he'd bent his head and his mouth was on hers.

The whole world stopped. It was as if a bolt of lightning had hit her, arrowing straight down her spine, rooting her to the spot.

Khalil was kissing her. Khalil was kissing *her*.

His fingers gripped her, pressing against her jaw, and she was tinder-dry grass, his mouth a flame, igniting her already smouldering desire and making it blaze into sudden, furious life.

A sigh of sheer relief escaped her, because she'd been waiting for this moment for ten years, hoping for it yet also knowing at the same time it would never come. Because he didn't feel that way about her. She'd told herself that so many times, and in the absence of any sign to the contrary she'd come to believe it.

Except apparently she'd been wrong all this time.

She was shaking as the reality of what was happening began to hit, and along with the relief came a dizzying wave of desire. All thought of pretending she wasn't affected by him, that she didn't still want him, vanished. The only thing that mattered was that she have more, get closer, because this was wasn't enough. It would *never* be enough.

Instinctively she lifted her hands, curling her fingers into the fine wool of his jacket, leaning into him. He was still, and for a terrible second she thought this would be that street in Soho all over again.

But then he moved again, pushing her up against the parapet and pinning her there with the hot length of his body. He was still cupping her cheek with one hand, and he shifted his thumb, pressing down on her bottom lip and opening her mouth to him, deepening the kiss.

Heat exploded between them, his tongue sweeping inside, devouring her as if she was a feast set before him and he was starving.

All conscious thought left her. There was only the press of his powerful body against hers, caging her against the stone. His hand slid from her jaw to the back of her head, cradling her as he kissed her harder, deeper.

Sometimes, alone in her college rooms at night, she'd allow herself to fantasise about what it would be like to kiss him or to have him kiss her, and she'd always thought it would be amazing. But the reality was better. Better than anything she could have possibly imagined.

This was what she'd been dreaming about for many years. His mouth on hers, kissing her as if he wanted her every bit as badly as she wanted him. And she *did* want him. She'd always wanted him and she probably always would.

What about your heart? You can't let him get this close...not again.

She wouldn't though. She knew how to protect herself. And anyway, this was just a kiss and she'd wanted a taste of him for so long. This was allowed, surely?

Her hands slid beneath his jacket, pressing against the white cotton of his shirt, feeling the iron-hard muscle and heat of his chest. He felt so good, warm and strong, and he smelled like heaven. Musk and sandalwood and exotic spices.

She'd missed him, she could admit that now. She'd missed him so much.

A helpless moan escaped her. She arched into him, the throb between her legs demanding, and, as if he knew exactly what she wanted, one hard thigh eased between hers, creating the most exquisite pressure.

She was a virgin. She'd never even been kissed before. But she knew what physical pleasure was and how to give it to herself, and yet the way he made her feel right now, even though he was barely touching her... It was more intense than anything she'd ever experienced. More intense than anything she could have imagined.

'Khal,' she whispered. 'Oh, please...'

His hand at the back of her head firmed and he kept her pinned against the parapet with his body. 'Come to Al Da'ira,' he murmured against her mouth. 'Give me two weeks. Two weeks to convince you to marry me. I will show you my country and my people. I will show you why I need you and only you.'

At first she barely heard him. Then gradually, through the haze of desire, the words penetrated.

He'd pulled back, lifting his mouth, his midnight gaze on hers. He didn't look away or try to hide the desire burning there. He let her see it.

It made her hot, made her heart flutter madly in her chest.

She could still feel his lips on hers, still taste his dark, heady flavour. And his body, rock-hard and tall and so broad... She'd never thought she'd have any of this. Never thought she'd have him look at her that way, have his kiss, have him want her.

'Two weeks?' She barely understood what she was saying herself, her voice husky, every part of her shaking.

'Yes, only two weeks.' He shifted, that hard thigh pressing insistently against her, right in the place she needed it most. His fingers pushed into her hair, tilting her head further back, and he lowered his mouth again, brushing it over hers. 'Only two weeks, *ya hayati*. You can stay in my palace, be waited on hand and foot, and I will give you everything it is in my power to give.'

Her senses reeled. 'Khal...'

'Please.' His voice warmed, became deeper, resonating with the part of her she'd always tried to keep closely guarded around him, and his lips moved over hers once again. 'Please, Sidonie.'

He'd never said 'please' to her before, never like this, with a note of demand and yet also with an echo of longing. As if he was desperate.

'I...'

'I will give you more of this.' His mouth explored lower, along her jawline. 'I will make you feel so very good.' He kissed a trail down her throat, his lips closing over her pulse. 'You have been waiting a long time for this, Sidonie. And so have I.'

He had? He'd been waiting, too?

The thought was there and then vanished, everything burning where he kissed her, as if he was scattering embers over her skin. Except instead of pain he left scorching pleasure, and all she could think was that she wanted more of it. Because he was right. She'd been waiting a long time for him and she was tired of it.

Why couldn't she have this? Have more of him? Two weeks of being in Al Da'ira, in his palace. Two weeks of being with him. She'd be careful, she wouldn't let herself get in too deep the way she had last time. And who knew, maybe it would even lay to rest a few ghosts?

He has to give you something too, though, and not just sex.

Yes. He could help with the charity, as she'd thought in the helicopter on the way here. He could be their royal patron, get them noticed, ensure they reached not just beyond the UK and into Europe, but globally too. There were so many orphaned children out there, children like her, children who needed help, and he could make a difference.

His mouth seared her tender throat, and she could feel the slight pressure of his tongue, the edge of his teeth. She closed her eyes, shivering in delight. 'You mentioned giving me something too,' she murmured. 'Something that I want, and I'm not talking about sex here.'

'I did.' His breath was warm against her skin. 'Name it.'

'You to lend your name to my charity. Be its patron. Help boost our profile.'

He answered without hesitation. 'I can do that.'

'Also, if I don't agree to marry you, I want to be free to leave. To go home.'

Another breath ghosted over her neck and then he commanded softly, 'Open your eyes.'

She did, automatically obeying him.

He'd lifted his head and was looking down at her, dark fire in his gaze. 'Yes, you will be free to leave. You have my word.'

Five years ago she would have trusted that word implicitly. But now... Well, he wasn't the same man she'd once known, he'd even admitted it himself. And she didn't know who this man was. She didn't know him at all.

An echo of grief made her throat close, grief for the friend who'd gone and left this man in his place. But grief wouldn't help. She had to be hard.

'Can I trust your word?' she made herself ask bluntly.

A flicker of something she couldn't decipher crossed his face and then was gone. 'You can. I swear to you on my crown.' His voice was flat and certain. 'And on the lives of my people.'

That meant something to him, she could tell. It was a vow.

'In that case,' she said, 'yes. I'll give you two weeks.'

CHAPTER FOUR

SIDONIE'S SKIN BENEATH his fingers was deliciously silky and warm, and Khalil didn't want to let her go. Her eyes had darkened into deep emerald and the pulse at the base of her throat, the pulse he'd just tasted, was racing.

He could hear his own blood roaring in his veins, desire like a giant heartbeat echoing inside him, and he could still taste her on his tongue, like summer, all honey and sunshine and sweetness.

He'd fantasised about how she'd taste many times, but the reality was better than any of his fantasies. He'd thought of kissing her many times, too, back when they'd been friends. Kissing her and more. But they'd remained just that, thoughts and fantasies. He'd kept his hands to himself no matter how difficult it had been.

Yet he hadn't been blind. He was an experienced man, and he knew when a woman wanted him. Sidonie had definitely wanted him back then and it seemed she still did, which was something he could use.

He hadn't wanted to. His mother's methods of using his emotions to teach him hard life lessons weren't ones he wanted to use on anyone else, let alone Sidonie. But he'd had to do something to get her agreement.

Putting his hand against her cheek had been calculated. He'd thought using her desire for him would aid his cause, but he hadn't expected the heat that had ignited inside him the moment he'd touched her.

He'd always wanted her, it was true, but his desire had felt like more than just want. It was as if the dam he kept between himself and his baser hungers had fractured, a dark and endless need welling up through the cracks, and he'd kissed her, pushed her up against that parapet before he'd fully understood what he was doing.

He had a longing not just for physical connection but also for her. For the woman he'd put out of his mind for so long that he'd thought she was gone for good. Except she hadn't gone. She was still there inside him, as was the ache of a loss he hadn't even realised he'd felt.

He hadn't been able to stop himself from deepening that kiss, from pushing her up against the parapet so he could feel her against him, her warmth settling into him. Easing the ache inside him. Her mouth beneath his had been so hot, like summer sun on his face after years of winter, and he'd had to force himself to remember what he was doing and what his goal was.

This wasn't about him and what he wanted.

This was about his country and his people, and no matter his pride. No matter that he'd never said please before in his life and certainly hadn't wanted to give her a two-week window in which to decide whether she wanted to marry him or not.

All that mattered was that she agreed.

So, he'd let her have it. Let her have his name for her charity too, because that was a small thing, and it wouldn't cost him anything, and it was clearly important to her. Two weeks wouldn't cost him either, would give her the illusion of choice at least, because at the end of that time he had no doubt at all that she'd marry him. He'd convince her. He'd use any and every weapon at his disposal if it meant she'd be his queen. His country demanded it.

Sensual pleasure would clearly be his weapon of choice, judging by the smoky green of her eyes, the delicate flush in her cheeks, and the way her full mouth had gone from firm to soft and pouty-looking.

Are you sure that is a good idea? Especially given your own response to her? You could become greedy, like Amir.

It was a concern, granted. Especially given his bloodline. But now he knew he was…susceptible, he'd be on his guard. He could control himself. His mother's lessons had been difficult, but he'd learned. And apart from all of that, he'd had five years of hardening himself into the King his people demanded. Of making sure the man he'd once been, the man full of doubts and flaws, was gone.

He could use their physical chemistry and not fall victim to it, he was certain.

She was staring up at him now from beneath her silky reddish lashes, and the temptation to kiss her again gripped him by the throat. But he mastered the urge. Instead he brushed his thumb over her mouth once more, relishing the give of her lower lip as he did so. 'Good. In that case, we leave tonight.'

Sidonie blinked. She was still pressed up against him, her fingers curled into the fabric of his jacket, and he was very, *very* conscious of the soft heat between her legs against his thigh and the press of her lush breasts against his chest.

You are hungry for her.

A physical hunger, nothing more. As a prince, after the nasty business of claiming his place in the succession was over, after his mother had died of the cancer that had taken hold of her, he'd let his desires run wild, let that poisonous blood have what it wanted, drowning the terrible doubt inside him about what he'd done. It had been before he'd met Sidonie and sex had been a good distraction.

But even then, his distractions had been calculated. His mastery over himself had never wavered, no matter how many women he took to his bed. And Sidonie, for all that she'd once meant to him, would be essentially just another woman.

Surprise crossed Sidonie's lovely face. 'Tonight? But…that's too soon.'

Khalil forced himself to release her jaw and step

back, which took more effort than it should. 'I am afraid I need to be back in Al Da'ira as soon as possible.'

The surprise vanished, that cool veneer slowly sliding back into place, hiding the sensual, sweet woman she'd been not a moment earlier. The real Sidonie. The Sidonie he remembered.

He didn't like that veneer. He didn't like it at all. Well, shattering it completely wouldn't take long. He wouldn't need two weeks to make his Sidonie return to him.

'That's unacceptable, Khalil,' she said. 'I told you. I have a business to run and people counting on me. I can't just up and leave with no notice.'

Thwarted desire coiled inside him, hot and demanding, eroding his patience and his temper along with it. He wasn't a man who gave in to such frustrations, but he was tired of fighting her. He had to get home. Already he'd wasted too much time coming to Paris and preparing a birthday meal that he hadn't even needed in the end. He should have just kissed her back in the pub in England.

'You will have to.' He didn't bother to hide the curt note in his voice. 'I cannot afford any more time away.'

Anger sparked in her gaze. 'Well, neither can I. If you need to get back, why don't you go and I can join you in a few—?'

'No,' he interrupted with all the steel of the King he was. 'You will be accompanying me and that is final.' She had to be with him when he arrived; that was non-negotiable. The correct form had to be observed if Sidonie was to be accepted as his queen, and for that she had to arrive with him.

'Why? What's wrong with our arriving separately?'

She was standing far too close to him and he couldn't help but notice that his fingers had pulled some silky red curls from her bun. They drifted around her neck, drawing attention to her pale, creamy skin and the tender hollow of her throat. A couple of buttons on her shirt were undone too and it would only take a couple of flicks of his fingers to open it completely and expose her to his gaze...

Desire tightened inside him once more, coiling and knotting, encouraging him to forget his control and take her here, now. Make her his. But he ignored it. This was not the right time or the right place, and he would do nothing to jeopardise their eventual marriage. No matter how much his body was urging him otherwise.

'We have certain customs that I must adhere to,' he said, forcing away the heat inside him.

'What customs? I'm just a visitor, Khalil, and presumably you don't have to accompany every visitor to Al Da'ira.'

If they kept going down this road they would have another argument, and yet more time would be wasted. His boundaries would be pushed and his temper further eroded. He couldn't allow that, not when he was on edge already.

'This is not up for discussion,' he said flatly, done

with the conversation. 'You may contact your people from the jet. Alternatively one of my staff will contact them on your behalf.'

It was clear she wasn't happy with that, because an angry flush had crept into her cheeks. 'I *run* the charity. You do remember that, don't you? I don't need "one of your staff" to contact my own employees.'

No, he hadn't remembered, and he should have, especially given all the discussions they'd had about her plans for starting a charity back in university. She'd been unsure of herself back then, but he'd encouraged her to follow her dreams. Because beneath that uncertainty she had drive and ambition, and he'd known she'd be brilliant at it.

He was annoyed with himself for forgetting, but his distance over the years had been deliberate, and there was no use regretting it. He'd made the decision to cut off all contact, and he couldn't go back and change it, even if he'd wanted to, which he didn't. He never second-guessed himself, never hesitated. Never let doubt undermine him. He couldn't afford to, not after Yusuf's death.

'Then you may contact them yourself,' he said. 'I do not care how you do it. But we *will* leave tonight regardless.'

Sidonie opened her mouth, but he carried on. 'One hour, Sidonie. Be ready.'

Then he strode past her and left her standing on the terrace staring after him.

CHAPTER FIVE

SIDONIE GROUND HER teeth with annoyance, watching Khalil's tall, broad figure disappear through the French doors.

She didn't like the man he'd become, not at all. He was insufferable.

'I knew my friend. I knew him very well, but you aren't him, are you?'

Her own words drifted back to her, as did his reply. *'No. Not any more.'*

That old grief pulsed inside her again, at the loss of the friend she'd once had. And it was clear that friend really had gone. But what she didn't understand was why.

What had happened to him? Why did Khalil feel he couldn't be him any more?

She turned away from staring at the door he'd just walked through, returning to the edge of the terrace and that view of Paris, trying to get a handle on the complicated mix of anger and loss that sat inside her.

He'd been so dismissive of her life and its requirements back in England. As if he hadn't sat with her all those nights in her rooms, going over her plans for the charity. Giving her advice and support, encouraging her. Believing in her.

Had he just…what? Forgotten about all of it? Forgotten that this had been her dream, and that he'd been a huge part in helping her find the confidence to reach for it?

The Khalil she remembered would never have forgotten. He wouldn't have swept grandly back into her life as if he still occupied the same space in it after five years of silence, either. The Khalil she remembered would have talked to her, would have listened to her concerns, and if she'd said no he'd have accepted it.

But as she'd told herself so many times already, as he'd even admitted himself, he wasn't that Khalil.

Can you blame him for putting his people and his country first?

No, she couldn't. He'd often told her that was what being a king was all about, the needs of his nation put before everything and everyone else, including himself. She'd thought it had sounded far too black and white, and that surely a king had to see to his own needs at some time, otherwise how could he look after everyone else? He'd accepted that, but even then, it was clear he didn't really believe it.

It seemed he didn't believe it now.

He wasn't going to matter to you, remember?

True. So why she was thinking about all the changes in him, she had no idea.

She leaned her elbows on the parapet and let out a

slow breath, conscious once again of the quick beat
of her heart and how sensitive her mouth felt. She
could still feel the pressure of his lips on hers, the
taste of him making her hungry, making her forget
what she'd told herself when he'd turned up only
hours before. That she wasn't going to let herself be
affected by him the way she had years ago. That she
was a different person now, a *stronger* person, who
didn't let her emotions run away with her.

*Yet you're still dropping everything to go to Al
Da'ira because he demanded it.*

No, that wasn't quite true. She *had* agreed to go,
but only after he'd said please and had agreed to be
her charity's patron. And she was only going for two
weeks. She hadn't agreed to his marriage demand,
either. She *had* resisted him, and if she wasn't much
mistaken she'd even got under his skin a little too.

Ahead of her the Eiffel Tower loomed, glittering
in the night.

She stared unseeingly at it, thinking about the
dark fire that had still been burning in his eyes after
that kiss.

*'You have been waiting a long time for this,
Sidonie. And so have I...'*

He'd been waiting, he'd said. Waiting a long time.
Which seem to indicate that maybe he hadn't been as
indifferent to her years ago as she'd thought.

A shiver went through her, a tight feeling settling
in her chest. She shouldn't be thinking of that. It
didn't matter what he'd felt for her back then, because

he'd never done anything about it. She'd tried to cross that line and he'd rebuffed her, for whatever reason.

Only the present mattered now.

Still. Maybe you're not so powerless against him after all.

The thought glowed in her head. Whatever he'd felt in the past, he wanted her now and that *was* a power she had, a power she'd never used or even understood, since no one had ever particularly wanted her before, not like that. And, while she wasn't sure how she could use it quite yet, she still had it.

Thinking about it gave her a little thrill. Because how many times had she ached for him over the years? Dreaming of the day he'd finally see her as not just a friend, but also as a woman he wanted. Yet at the same time knowing that day would never come, because he would never see her that way. Why would he? When no one else ever had?

But that day *had* come. Now, finally, he saw her as a woman. Finally she could make him burn for her. Make him ache for her, long for her. Make him as desperate for her as she'd been for him. That would be fair, wouldn't it?

But can you? Or will you end up making yourself his slave once again?

Sidonie focused once more on the Eiffel Tower, all iron, hard metal to withstand the centuries.

Back when she'd been a kid she'd learned how to be quiet and undemanding, moulding herself into the perfect niece for her aunt, a good girl who never caused a fuss and never drew attention to herself.

Then she'd met Khalil, his intensity demanding something from her, something that living with Aunt May had forced her to keep down deep inside. An intensity of her own that she'd kept locked away, a passion and drive she hadn't known she'd had. He'd encouraged it, made it flourish. Being with him had felt as though she could breathe for the first time in her life. Then had come the mistake she'd made, his painful departure, and that email breaking off all contact. And the part of her that he'd unlocked, she'd had to put away again.

It had been a hard lesson to learn but she'd learned it. She'd never want anything from anyone, never open herself to anyone. She'd found the iron inside her, armour to protect herself. She visited her aunt when it suited her and only because May wasn't in good health these days, and besides, staying away would have meant May still had the power to hurt her and she didn't.

As for Khalil, well… He'd soon discover she wasn't as malleable as she'd once been, if he hadn't already.

'Miss Sullivan?'

Sidonie turned to find a woman in a black uniform standing behind her. 'Yes?'

'Your car to the airport is here. His Majesty also wishes to inform you that you will not need any luggage. He will see to anything you require personally.'

Behind the woman Sidonie could see other servants busily packing up the carefully set table and blowing out all the candles. Since she'd agreed to come with him, the birthday dinner clearly wasn't needed any more.

That gave her a slight stab of hurt, but she ignored it. The important thing was she'd got his agreement to help her charity and that mattered more than any silly birthday dinner. Anyway, she'd go to Al Da'ira and enjoy a pleasant two weeks' holiday, perhaps lose her virginity to him, lay those old ghosts, and then she'd come back to England and she'd *never* think of him again.

The trip from the private mansion to a private airfield just out of Paris, where Khalil's jet waited, wasn't long. She'd thought when she got into the car that he would be there too and was surprised when he wasn't. He wasn't on the tarmac when she reached the airfield, nor waiting by the sleek black jet with the gleaming gold tail livery.

She wondered if he was already inside, but after she'd climbed the stairs and stepped into the plane the series of small rooms she was led through were empty. The interior was all luxurious cream leather and gleaming dark wood, and the seat she was taken to was more a recliner than an aircraft seat, deep and enveloping her in comfort as soon as she sat down.

There was still no sign of him and she was beginning to wonder what was going on, when she heard his deep voice coming from the jet's doors, towards the nose of the plane. He was speaking in his beautiful, melodic language, and despite herself her heartbeat sped up.

It was ridiculous. It hadn't even been an hour since

he'd walked off the terrace and already she was excited at the thought of seeing him again. Not a good
sign when she should be trying to ring Bethany, her
personal assistant, to let her know she was having
an unexpected break and to reschedule her meetings,
plus check to make sure she didn't have any events
planned for the next two weeks.

Except all she did was sit there, staring at the entrance of the little sitting area she was in, waiting
for him to arrive.

But he didn't.

Even after the jet had taken off and they were at
cruising altitude, he didn't show.

She made her calls, Bethany assuring her that a
sudden two-week holiday was no problem at all, and
in fact Sidonie probably needed it, so she wasn't to
worry about anything.

Sidonie found it a little disconcerting that two
weeks could pass without her being needed, but,
since she was already in the air and flying to her
destination, there wasn't much she could do about it
but be glad it wasn't a problem.

She'd need to tell her team about his being on
board to be patron, but she could do that once she
had a formal agreement from him.

It was an overnight flight and, after dinner had
been served and she'd eaten, a steward showed her to
a bedroom that included a king-sized bed with luxurious white sheets for her to sleep in. She wondered
if she should refuse on principle, but then decided

that was silly. She was officially on holiday now and so why not avail herself of a bed in a private jet?

Khalil still hadn't appeared and she worried that she wasn't going to sleep while obsessing about him, but she must have been more tired than she thought, because she fell asleep as soon as her head hit the pillow.

She slept like the dead and the next thing she knew she was being woken by a stewardess, who told her that they were two hours out of Al Da'ira, and that she could avail herself of the bathroom facilities, which included a shower. His Majesty had also provided fresh clothes for her to wear. Because of course he had.

Sidonie stared at the dress that had been laid out on the small couch near the bed, the leaf-green silk contrasting vividly with the cream of the leather. It was beautiful, designed to wrap around her torso before flowing out into full, floaty skirts that dropped from her hips.

Her throat tightened, aching suddenly. She should be irritated at him for again arrogantly providing her with clothing that she had no doubt would fit perfectly, as would the lacy green silk bra and knickers that had also been provided. But she wasn't.

The lonely child she'd once been had never had anything bought for her. She'd had to wear clothes that were too small and shoes that were too tight, because her aunt hadn't noticed her growing. And even when Sidonie had told her that she couldn't fit into her clothes any more, her aunt had acted as if she was making a fuss over nothing. There had never been birthday presents. Never been Christmas presents. Only the bare minimum had been provided and she was expected to be grateful.

But this…this was not the bare minimum. This dress was beautiful, in a colour she loved, and in her size. It had been bought specifically for her.

He thought of you. He remembered.

Her chest tightened as another memory drifted through her head. Of that twenty-first birthday party Khalil had arranged for her, and how she hadn't been expecting presents, since she never got anything, not for her birthday.

The party itself had been so wonderful and dancing with him more wonderful still, and she'd thought nothing could top it. Then, after everyone had gone, Khalil had given her a birthday present. It was a dainty necklace that consisted of a simple gold chain with a golden sun that sat in the hollow of her throat.

'Because you are sunshine, Sidonie,' he'd said. *'My sunshine.'*

She'd fallen in love with him in that moment. For the party he'd organised for her and the touching present he'd given her. She'd loved him for how he'd known what it would mean to her, and that she hadn't had to ask. Because her whole life up to that point had been having to ask for everything. And being afraid to.

Khalil had never made her feel afraid to ask. Not once.

And look what happened. Being cut dead on a snowy Soho street.

Oh, yes, she remembered. And the next day she'd thrown his necklace in the rubbish.

The memory was too painful, so she pushed it away, taking a shower instead and putting on the silky underwear and the beautiful dress. And indeed, when she looked at herself in the mirror, not only was it a perfect fit, but it also suited her. The colour accentuated her red hair and brought out the green in her eyes.

She debated briefly, putting her hair up into its usual bun, but then decided that, since she was on holiday, she was going to leave it loose.

He might like it like that.

Yes. He might. And she could use that perhaps.

Satisfied with her appearance, Sidonie stepped out of the bedroom and went into the lounge area.

And stopped dead.

Khalil was sitting on one of the couches, his arms resting along the back, long, powerful legs stretched out in front of him and crossed at the ankles. He wore a black suit and a black shirt with a silk tie of many different shades of green.

Sidonie's heart leapt into her throat, her mouth going dry.

He was absolutely mesmerising.

And he was looking straight at her.

Khalil had been waiting for Sidonie to wake up for a good ten minutes and, while he'd tried for patience, this time he found each passing second a trial. He hadn't slept during the flight and he'd purposefully not visited her since they'd taken off either.

He'd had a lot of work to do and didn't want to waste time sleeping, and he'd also decided that the key to her agreeing to marrying him would be to keep her hungry for him and his presence.

You wouldn't have been able to sleep anyway. Not after that kiss.

Khalil ignored the thought. He'd never allowed his hungers to affect him in such a way and he wasn't going to start now.

Yet the moment Sidonie stepped out of the plane's bedroom, glowing in the green silk gown he'd had made especially for her, all he was aware of was his hunger.

Green had always been his favourite colour on her. It made her skin seem pale as cream and drew emerald sparks from her eyes.

She'd used to wear a loose, silky green blouse almost exactly the same colour as the gown she wore now, and it had been his favourite. Once, when she'd invited him out to dinner at a restaurant one evening with some of her friends, she'd leaned across him to get something, and the fabric had brushed against his bare arm. He'd been transfixed. All he'd been able to think about was whether her skin would feel as soft and silky as her blouse, and how he wanted to find out.

She'd only been his friend for a couple of months

at that stage, but that had been the first moment he'd realised he wanted her.

He could feel that want now, sparking in the air between them, along with an intense satisfaction that she'd put on the dress he'd bought for her and that she looked as beautiful in it as he'd thought she would.

No. She looked better. She was perfection. Exactly how he'd wanted her to look as he brought her back to his country as his bride. Bright and beautiful and all wrapped in green, like a spring morning. A sign of hope and a kinder, gentler change.

He didn't move for a second, taking her in.

A flush stained her lovely cheeks, but her gaze was cool. Clearly, the veneer was back in place. It didn't matter. Tonight he would shatter it once more, or at least put a few more cracks in it, and by the end of the two weeks she'd allowed, it would be gone completely. And his Sidonie would finally be what she'd always meant to be: his.

She is supposed to be for your country, not for you.

Well, of course. But he could have a small piece of her for himself. It was only physical hunger, and she would be his wife. Heirs had to be got somehow.

'Thank you for the dress, Khalil.' Her voice was as cool as her gaze. 'It's beautiful. But it's really more suitable for a ball than getting off a plane.'

'The arrival of my intended bride requires some ceremony.' He got to his feet, unable to stop staring at her and the way the gown wrapped around her, clinging to the generous curves of her breasts, waist and hips. 'And green is the colour of change.'

Her red brows drew together. 'But I'm not your intended bride. I told you that I was—'

'*You* have decided that you are not,' he interrupted gently. 'But *my* decision remains. You are the bride I have chosen and I will announce you as such.'

Her chin firmed, little sparks of anger glittering deep in her eyes. She was holding it back. He could see that now. Her veneer was not perfect. 'So what happens when I leave? After you've made such a big song and dance about me?'

He shrugged. 'Then you will leave.'

'But what will your people think? After you've told them that I'm going to be your queen?'

'I thought it did not matter,' he said silkily, 'because they are not your people.'

She reddened. 'No, but I don't want to be presented as something I'm not. It's a bit too much like lying for comfort.'

'If it makes you feel any better, I am not lying to my people. I truly believe that you will be my intended bride.'

'But I don't, Khalil. I don't believe that.'

The thing inside him, the predator, shifted. The way she challenged him excited him, the way it had always excited him. He was used to people doing whatever he said and certainly no one argued with him, and the fact that Sidonie was resisting him at every turn both annoyed and fascinated him.

She'd done the same back when they'd been

friends, refusing to bow to his arrogance and always calling him out on it.

'You're being ridiculous, Khal,' she'd say, laughing. *'You're not a prince here, remember?'*

He wasn't, and he'd loved that, and that was why part of him had never wanted to leave England. Never wanted to leave her. The thought of returning to Al Da'ira to eventually take his crown, be a king, had seemed at times...unbearable.

She's dangerous. Remember that.

She had been back then, because back then there had been some softness in him. But that softness had gone. He'd cut it out of himself, along with that longing to stay in England with her. There was no longing now, and she was no longer a threat.

He shrugged. 'Then we will have an interesting two weeks, will we not?'

Something flashed in Sidonie's gaze, another challenge, and he felt that terrible part of him shift once again in response.

But he forced it back in its cage. He would not let it out. Not again.

'Come,' he said calmly. 'You need breakfast, and we land in an hour.'

She eyed him suspiciously but let herself be guided to a seat, and when breakfast was brought to them she ate with him. He'd already decided not to tell her about the custom of the Kings of Al Da'ira when it came to their brides, of carrying them into the new home they would share. The custom went back centuries, harking back to the days when the desert warriors went on raids to capture their wives, and, while Khalil was hell-bent on changing some of those customs, it wouldn't hurt to observe a few to ease the pain of too much change, too quickly.

She might not be happy with him carrying her, but the lack of sleep was catching up with him, and he was tired. He didn't want her to argue, not right now, and besides, a part of him wanted this very much. The part that had fantasised about a life that didn't involve his being a king. Where he was just a man and Sidonie was the woman he loved. Where he held her in his arms, nestled against his chest, and he carried her into the home they would share.

He would never be that man again, but he could indulge himself a little in that fantasy now, couldn't he? It didn't mean losing control of his baser appetites or admitting to any weaknesses. It was…merely appeasing old ghosts.

Anticipation gathered inside him as the breakfast was cleared away and the plane began its descent. Sidonie was gazing out of the window at the countryside unrolling beneath them, the vast mountains and wide deserts of his homeland. A stark and harsh land, but incredibly beautiful.

Once he'd stabilised the country, he had plans for a big tourism push, to share Al Da'ira with the world. It was already a rich nation due to the oil, but his family's greedy hands had kept it for themselves, and so he'd also planned to redistribute that wealth amongst the wider populace. Once his people had food and good housing, they could then turn their attention to new business ventures such as tourism.

Survival mode was not good for anyone, as he knew all too well.

The plane descended then came in for a perfect landing on the private airstrip reserved for the royal family, and already he could see the usual entourage waiting to welcome their King back to his country.

That too involved a specific custom.

As his staff prepared to open the plane door, Khalil got to his feet, then reached out a hand to Sidonie, sitting opposite. She took it automatically and he could feel her stiffen as his fingers closed around her smaller ones, gathering them into his palm. Her eyes had gone wide, her luscious mouth opening.

No wonder. He could feel the electricity where their skin touched, a cascade of sparks igniting every nerve ending. Desire shifted and tightened, his body hardening in response, and he pulled her closer, looking down into her darkening green eyes and seeing his own desire mirrored back at him.

Tonight. He would do something about it tonight.

'What are you doing?' she asked huskily. 'I thought we were getting off the plane.'

'We are.' He let go of her hand, and before she had a chance to move away he picked her up and gathered her close against his chest. 'But as I said, there are certain customs I must follow.'

She'd gone rigid in his arms, her eyes widening. 'Khalil—'

'And one of those customs involves carrying my intended bride into the home we will share. My country is my home, therefore I will be carrying you from the plane to the car that will take us back to the palace.'

She glared at him, her body stiff. 'And as *I* said, I never agreed to be your intended bride.'

He tightened his grip, even though she hadn't moved, because she was warm and soft against his chest and he wanted to keep her there. 'Tell me you don't like being in my arms, Sidonie.' He stared down into her angry green eyes. 'Tell me you don't like being close to me. Make me believe it, and maybe I will let you walk to the car instead.'

Her mouth was a firm line, but then she looked away. 'You can have your custom.' A delicate pink flush stained her cheekbones. 'I don't want to offend your people.'

His satisfaction deepened. It wasn't about giving offence to his people, no matter what she said. She liked being in his arms, that was the truth.

'Of course not,' he murmured, turning towards the door. 'Though nothing you do could give offence.'

'I'm sure that's not true.'

He glanced down at her.

She was staring out of the open doorway of the plane, to the bright sun, the stark mountains, and the crowd of people standing on the tarmac ready to welcome them. There was a crease between her brows, her body tense where it rested against his, trepidation clear on her face.

'There is nothing you need to do,' he said, wanting to reassure her. 'You are here as my chosen one and as such you will be accepted without question.'

She glanced up at him and just like that the trepidation vanished, the cool veneer sliding once more back into place. 'And why is that? Because no one questions you?'

'Yes,' he said simply. 'The King has to be above question.'

Her mouth opened, no doubt to tell him something he didn't particularly want to hear, but it was time to exit the plane, and so he stepped through the doors and went down the stairs, Sidonie in his arms.

The most important members of his court were there, as he'd instructed them to be. They'd protested at his choice of potential queen, but he'd ignored them. He would have his way in this. He *would* change his country for the better.

He wouldn't let the death of Yusuf, the half-brother he'd defeated, have been for nothing.

Almost as one, the arrayed servants and members of his court dropped to their knees and prostrated themselves as he stepped off the stairs and onto the tarmac.

Sidonie's eyes went wide. 'I kind of didn't believe you when you told me that the Kings are semi-divine here.'

'I take it you do now.' He strode through the crowd

of servants and nobility, towards the long black limo that waited for them.

He didn't look at her, but he could feel her sharp gaze on him. 'Yes, I do,' she said. 'But what puzzles me is why you keep letting them believe that.'

They were nearing the car now, Al Da'ira's hot sun burning down on them even though it was still early in the morning.

'I do not let them believe anything,' he replied. 'My people make their own choices. However, their confidence in the crown was shaken by my father, and it is my job to give them back that confidence. Confidence that I am not the same as him.'

'But surely they can see that already?'

He glanced down, finding her clear green eyes staring back. 'They considered Amir just a man because he was so flawed. A king, on the other hand, must be without flaw. He must be more than a man, and so that is what I must be. It is a belief that will have to change some day and I will change it. But now is not the time. There are still too many scars left by my father.'

'I see.' Sidonie's voice was quiet, her gaze oddly searching. 'That's quite the standard you hold yourself to.'

For some reason the simple observation felt like a pressure against the piece of rock that was his heart. A pressure he had to ignore. It was a flaw that he thought he'd got rid of years ago.

They were at the car now and he paused as a servant leapt up from the tarmac to pull open the door, and then glanced down at the woman in his arms.

Her expression was difficult to interpret, but he was sure that the green sparks in her eyes weren't caused by anger now. She put a hand on his chest. 'Khalil.'

But whatever she was going to say, he didn't want to hear it. Didn't want to put any more pressure on that flaw. Besides, now wasn't the time for discussion. He had to be welcomed formally by his staff and then he would have a debrief from his advisors. That was likely to take a while, and if he didn't get to it now he wouldn't have time with her afterwards. And he wanted that time.

'Later,' he said. 'You will be going to the palace now.' He took a step to the open door of the limo and deposited her inside it.

'Wait.' Her fingers closed on his jacket, gripping tight, and that trepidation had crept back into her eyes again. 'You're not coming with me?'

The way she held on to him reminded him of too many things. Of that night in Soho, when she'd held on to his coat the way she was doing now, her green eyes full of painful hope. And he'd wanted more than anything for that beautiful mouth of hers to meet his and to hear the words no one had ever said to him before. *I love you.* And to say them back.

But he hadn't been able to then because he'd had a duty, and he still had that duty. Nothing had changed. He still was what he was, and those were words he could never say.

Love was not and never had been permitted to kings.

'I am not.' Gently he pulled her fingers from his jacket and because, after all, he couldn't help himself, he turned her palm up in his and bent to brush a kiss over it. 'But you will be well taken care of back at the palace and I will see you tonight.'

For a moment she just looked at him and he couldn't tell what she was thinking. Then she gave a nod, pulled her hand from his, and turned away.

CHAPTER SIX

SIDONIE STOOD BY the pool in the atrium that lay in the centre of what was the Queens' wing of Al Da'ira's royal palace.

The pool had been beautifully made with swirling patterns of blue, green, and gold tiles, its clear blue water full of glittering koi fish. There were water lilies here and there, the flowers open and filling the air with a delicate scent.

In the arcade surrounding the pool were shrubs in pots and at one end a fountain played. The light from the setting sun came through the glass that covered the atrium, painting the white marble floor with gold and red and pink.

It was beautiful.

In fact, the whole palace was beautiful, though she hadn't had a chance to explore it, not when most of her day since being transported from the airport to the palace had involved being introduced to the various staff members who'd be looking after her and then being shown around the Queens' wing.

That was beautiful too. It was a series of intercon-

nected, white-tiled rooms with high, arched windows
that gave magnificent views out over Al Da'ira's capital city, the mountains that surrounded it, as well as
glimpses into private little courtyards full of fountains and orange trees.

There was a big, white-curtained bed piled high
with pillows and a huge bathroom with a shower
big enough for five people, as well as a vast bath
carved from white marble veined with gold and set
on a plinth. The rooms also contained a comfortable
sitting room, a library, a small, private swimming
pool with a waterfall at one end, and a gym with all
the latest fitness machines. The palace staff member
who had been assigned to her, a lovely woman in her
late forties called Aisha, had also proudly showed
her a study with everything she needed to work remotely, including a broadband connection, a desktop
computer, and a sleek little laptop.

Everything was provided, including a wardrobe
full of clothes and luxurious toiletries.

And tonight, Aisha had informed her, she'd be
dining with His Majesty.

Sidonie swallowed, adjusting the neckline of the
cocktail gown she was wearing. She'd wanted to stay
in the green dress that she'd worn coming off the
plane, but the moment she'd settled into her apartments Aisha had directed her to the wardrobe and
had brought out the gown the King wanted her to
wear for their dinner tonight.

It was in gold silk and floor-length, with a deep
vee neckline that plunged between her breasts, al-

most to her navel, and long, flowing sleeves. The skirts were loose and flowing too. It would have been modest if not for that neckline.

She loved it. Gold wasn't a colour she had ever imagined wearing, but its rich tones made her skin gleam and her hair seem even redder, and that deep neckline… She wasn't able to wear a bra with it.

All that was missing, her brain reminded her helpfully, was the little gold necklace he'd given her for her twenty-first, the one she'd thrown away after he'd left her.

But there was no point thinking about that. The necklace was gone, part of the past she'd chosen to leave behind. And really, did she need it?

When she'd stepped out of the bedroom on the plane she'd seen blatant hunger leap in his eyes, and she'd felt fully the power of her sexuality. She'd once dreamed of him staring at her like that and he had, and it had been just as exhilarating, dizzying even, as she'd imagined. She'd wished she'd had more time to work out what she could do with it, but then there had been breakfast and they'd landed, and he'd pulled her into his arms and carried her from the plane.

She hadn't been entirely happy about that, because he hadn't warned her it would happen. Then he'd called her out on how much she liked being close to him and she hadn't been able to deny it.

He'd held her before, back when they'd been friends—that wasn't unusual. Hugs to greet one another and to say goodbye. Hugs of congratulation or commiseration. Hugs of comfort when the anniversary of her parents' death came around and she grieved the family she'd lost.

But the way he'd held her as they'd disembarked the plane had been different. He'd felt different. His chest had been broader and harder, his arms powerful and steady, and it hadn't been anything like those long-ago hugs. The intensity in his eyes as he'd looked down at her had stolen her breath. There had been a triumph of sorts in them, as if she was a prize he'd won, and yes, she'd liked it.

Being close to him had been as intoxicating as it had been in Paris, and she'd found herself staring up at the sharp, stern lines of his beautiful face. Lines that hadn't been there years ago, she was sure of it. The sight had made something inside her ache.

His expression was so hard, like granite, and all his court with their faces pressed to the tarmac.

'A king, on the other hand, must be without flaw. He must be more than a man, and so that is what I must be.'

Why did he think that? He'd mentioned his father as an example of flawed humanity, and she knew he was trying not to follow his example, but... Did he really think he had to be more than a man? And was it really for the sake of his people or for his own? As she'd told him, it was such a high standard to hold himself to.

'Miss Sullivan?'

Sidonie looked up from her contemplation of the fish pool, shoving away the ache that had somehow crept into her heart.

A servant in the black and gold of the palace livery was standing in the doorway to the atrium. He bowed. 'His Majesty requests the pleasure of your company. You are to follow me, please.'

It wasn't a request. It was an order. And if she hadn't been distracted by thinking of Khalil, she might have been annoyed by it. But she was distracted. She couldn't stop seeing the expression on his face as he'd carried her to the car. It had been so rigid. Then, as she'd gripped his jacket when she'd realised he wasn't coming with her, a sudden anxiety sitting in her gut, she'd seen that rigidity ripple, the look in his eyes softening almost imperceptibly. Then he'd kissed her hands.

The man you knew isn't gone. He's still in there somewhere.

Sidonie's heart ached a little more as she followed the servant from the Queens' apartments and into the main palace wing. The marble floors were veined with gold and the walls were tiled in all kinds of patterns and in all kinds of colours, including glittering metallic silver and gold.

Did it matter if her friend was still there? Was that man still important to her? He'd been gone so long, and she'd changed so much. Did she really want to find him again? Connect with him again? After all her heart had suffered? Or was it easier only to deal with the stranger, the King he'd become?

She was only here for two weeks, after all, and she *would* leave at the end of it. And even if she did manage to find the friend she'd loved, what then?

You'd have married him. You wanted *to marry him.*

A shiver went through her. It was true, she had. That was why she'd insisted on that marriage promise. But now? She didn't know. Khalil her friend might still exist in Khalil the King, but did the old Sidonie still exist in her? And if she did, would she want to become her again? Let her heart get broken again?

You can't. You must protect yourself.

She did, yet... That ache inside her, that longing, was stronger now than it had ever been, even though she'd told herself she didn't feel it. The ache that told her she was a liar and that, while protecting herself was all well and good, it hadn't made her any happier.

Can you even remember the last time you were happy?

She tried not to think about that as they came to a stop outside a pair of massive gilded double doors. The King's wing of the palace. Ceremonial guards in black and gold uniforms were stationed outside and they regarded Sidonie without expression, allowing her and the servant to step through into the King's private apartments.

They were just as lushly tiled, though the furnishings were spare, perhaps to draw attention to the colours and swirling patterns of the tiles.

Eventually they stopped outside a simple door of dark wood. The man knocked once and then opened the door, gesturing to Sidonie to go inside.

Her heart gave a sudden hard beat, a fluttering

feeling way down deep in her gut. A whisper of the old excitement that had used to grip her every time they met.

He still makes you feel like a love-sick teenager.

He did, oh, he did. And maybe she was a fool for still feeling this way so many years later, but she couldn't help it, just as she couldn't deny she felt it.

Taking a moment to steady herself, Sidonie then stepped through the doorway, the door closing softly behind her.

It was a small room and intimate, with more doors that stood open onto a perfect little courtyard. A fountain sat in the centre of the courtyard, filling the air with gentle music. The walls of the room were lined with bookshelves and on the floor were silken rugs in rich reds and deep blues. Low couches upholstered in pale linen stood grouped around an unlit fireplace and a low table in dark wood.

Khalil sat on one of the couches, reading something on a tablet, which he put down the moment the door opened.

He was dressed very simply, in a black robe embroidered with gold and loose black trousers. His chest was bare.

Her mouth dried completely.

She'd never seen him in anything but Western clothing, the jeans and T-shirt of a student, and then later a series of perfectly tailored, handmade suits. He'd been gorgeous in those, but dressed in the clothing of his country, with all that muscled bronze skin on show… God, he was stunning.

The sharp, predatory angles of his face seemed sharper somehow, his black eyes even blacker. He was every inch the regal, mesmerising, charismatic King.

Yet there was a part of her, a tiny, forgotten part, that felt a stab of disappointment. As if she'd wanted him to be someone else.

He rose as the door closed behind her, his intense gaze finding hers. 'Good evening, *ya hayati*. I hope you were well looked after today and that the accommodation is to your liking.'

Sidonie clasped her hands together in front of her, trying to keep her gaze from the broad expanse of his chest. Then she caught the gleam in his eyes as he watched her and realised suddenly that he'd done it on purpose. He was trying to tempt her, wasn't he? He was showing her what she could have if she married him.

You can't deny that you want it.

Oh, yes, she did. But sex wasn't enough of an inducement.

How would you know when you haven't had it?

'Yes,' she said, ignoring the voice in her head. 'The accommodation is perfect, actually. Though, I have to say, it's huge.'

'It would be. The Queens' wing was for queens, plural.'

Ah, yes, so it would. Khalil had told her that Amir had had four wives. He'd been the only child of wife number three and had been brought up in a house in the mountains, not at court.

'Your mother didn't live there, did she?' Sidonie asked, curious.

'No. She never wanted to. She preferred our house in the mountains.'

He'd told her of that house, with lots of gardens and trees, though his life there hadn't exactly been idyllic. There had been lots of rigorous schooling, he'd said, and physical training, and not much time for playing. No time for friends, either.

Hers had been the same, at least the school and friends part of it. Her aunt hadn't allowed her to have friends back because she hadn't wanted any 'shouting and screaming'. And Sidonie hadn't gone to other kids' houses because she hated asking her aunt to take her. Sometimes May would, but she always acted as if it were a huge imposition.

'Why?' Sidonie asked. 'Didn't she like living with the other wives?'

'She did not. She fell out of favour with my father anyway and he had her sent away.'

'Oh? Why was that?'

'She did not like the way he acted, and she was not afraid to tell him so. She also wanted to protect me.' Khalil's eyes gleamed. 'Do not worry, Sidonie. I will not be having more than one wife, I told you that.'

Sidonie had heard the horror stories of the battle of succession, a custom where the oldest children of each queen would fight a ritualistic battle for the right to be named heir. Long ago there had been assassination attempts on children and their mothers to take them out of the running, Khalil had told her, and that sometimes it still happened.

She knew Khalil had wanted to change that, since his own battle had involved wounding his half-brother, Yusuf, badly enough that Yusuf had had to concede the crown. She'd been appalled when he'd told her about it, instantly afraid for him, and had wanted to ask more questions, but he'd changed the subject. And since it had been clearly a painful memory, she hadn't pushed him.

But…would he tell her now if she asked? Would it still be painful for him? Or was this all he was? This hard, cold king who looked as if he'd never known a moment's pain in all his life?

'What is it?' Khalil asked, his deep voice dark and smooth. 'You are looking at me very intently.'

And she answered without thought. 'I'm wondering what happened to my friend, Khalil.'

Sidonie stood there in the golden gown he'd chosen for her and she was every bit as beautiful in it as she'd been in the green dress she'd worn on the plane. She was glowing almost, the gold fabric making her look as if she'd been bathed in sunlight. Her red hair was in a simple, loose ponytail that hung over her shoulder and curled down over her chest, drawing attention to the deep neckline and the shadowed curves of her breasts.

He'd been looking forward to this moment all day. The moment when he'd finally be alone with her and he could start the business of convincing her to say yes to his marriage proposal.

He'd prepared and his preparations were thorough.

A special meal would be brought here, to his favourite room, which he often used when he needed some time alone, along with some of Al Da'ira's finest wines. And while they ate, he'd talk to her about all the benefits of being his wife. Then after that he'd continue with the seduction he'd initiated back in Paris, demonstrate those benefits physically.

In fact, he was thinking that maybe he'd seduce her first, before the dinner. He was finding it difficult to pay attention to what she was saying, too distracted by the sight of her.

'Your friend?' he asked impatiently. 'I told you. He is gone.'

'Why?'

'Because he was not the man to rule this country.'

A crease deepened between her brows. 'I don't understand. I thought he'd have made an excellent king.'

The pressure in his chest, the one that had gripped him that morning as he'd put her in the car, intensified. Why was she talking about this? Their friendship had been precious, a long golden summer in the middle of a harsh winter, but it was gone now. It was over, and the man he'd once been had gone along with it, and that man wasn't coming back.

'He was not strong enough,' Khalil said. 'I told you; a king must be more than a man.' Gesturing at the couch, he went on, 'Come and sit with me, *ya hayati*. I will pour you a glass of wine and you can tell me about your charity while we wait for our meal.'

She gave him a considering look and he thought she might not let it go, but then she came over to the couch and sat down, the neckline of her golden gown shifting, giving him the most intriguing glimpse of the shadowed valley between her breasts. It was obvious that she was not wearing a bra.

His heartbeat accelerated, sudden and intense desire gripping him. It would be so easy to seduce her right here on the couch, to have her naked and beneath him, to be inside her. It wouldn't take him long. She wanted him. The way she kept looking very pointedly everywhere except at his chest told its own story and that was as he'd hoped.

You are too impatient.

Yes, that was true. But he'd waited a long time to have her. And no matter what he thought about the man he'd been, that man's memories still filled his head.

Of Sidonie looking up at him the night he'd given her that necklace for her twenty-first. A sun because she'd been sunshine to him. There had been tears in her eyes along with a bright, painful emotion that had caught him by the throat. She'd looked at him as if he'd given her the moon and all the stars, and he'd wanted to kiss her right then and there. Wanted to tell her that he meant it, that she was the only sun in his sky. Because after Yusuf's death, he'd been able to see nothing but darkness.

Except he hadn't kissed her, and he hadn't told her, because he couldn't back then. He hadn't wanted to start something he wouldn't be able to finish.

But things were different now. She wasn't his sun any more—he didn't need sunshine to survive these days—but she was still every bit as beautiful, every bit as desirable as she'd been back then. And now he could kiss her. Now he could do more than that, and he wanted to. He *wanted* to.

She was fussing with her dress, pulling at the neckline, and, since he was still standing, he found his gaze settling on the curves of her breasts and the pale, creamy skin revealed by the fabric.

Her gaze lifted to his suddenly and he didn't look away. Didn't make any attempt to pretend he had been looking anywhere else but at her and the beauty of her body.

A flush rose into her cheeks, but she didn't look away either. Her eyes darkened as the space between them became full of a crackling tension, all the aching years of desire and the pull of a longing he'd deliberately cut out of his heart.

Are you sure it isn't still there?

No, of course it wasn't. The longing he felt now was only physical.

'Why did you go?' she asked abruptly. 'Why did you walk away from me that night?'

It was the very last question he'd expected and the very last question he wanted to answer. Though he should have known she'd ask at some point. And he had to tell her. She had to understand what he was now. Who he was now.

'I had to.' His voice was rougher than he wanted it to be. 'I was always going to leave, Sidonie. I had a country to rule. Al Da'ira was my responsibility, and I could not walk away from it.'

'But I told you I loved you, Khalil. And you just… left.'

The pressure inside him climbed. He knew he'd been abrupt, knew that his sudden dismissal of her had hurt her, but it was either that or drag her into his arms, which would have been equally hurtful.

'Yes,' he said. 'What you told me was a shock and I did not…know how to deal with it.'

Her expression was painful in its honesty. 'Was me loving you so very bad?'

'No, of course not.' The tight feeling in his chest made him ache. 'But… I could not love you in return, Sidonie, though I very much wanted to. All I could do was walk away.'

There was a kind of anguish in her eyes that felt like a knife to his heart, and some part of him was disturbed by it and the pressure inside him. She shouldn't still have the power to affect him like this. She shouldn't.

'And that email?' There was pain in her voice. 'Did you really have to tell me not to contact you again?'

There was pain inside him too now, seeking the flaw in the stone, trying to crack him apart. But he was harder than that these days. Far too hard. He had tempered himself in the fire his mother had built for him, to protect him, and now nothing could get through. Not even her.

'Yes.' He held her gaze, letting her see who he was now. What he would always be. 'I sent you that email because the friend I was to you, the friend you remembered… I could no longer be him. And I thought it was better that you forget me.'

Her green eyes darkened still further, becoming the colour of deep jungle forests, full of shadows. 'I don't understand, Khalil. You know, I wasn't asking you to love me back. I just wanted to tell you how I felt. And I get that it was a shock. But dismissing five years of close friendship because…what? You didn't want to be my friend any more? That I don't get at all.'

The ache in his chest twisted. He didn't know why he still felt it, why it was still there after all these years when it shouldn't be. Memories, yes, he could do nothing about those, but that ache, that longing, that *feeling*…

Feelings were not allowed. They never had been. His mother had taught him that and he'd learned those lessons well.

'It was not that I did not want to, Sidonie,' he said flatly. 'I could not. Love, friendship…they are not allowed for a king. Yes, I could have remained in contact. I could have continued to visit England. But I was not the man you remembered, and I thought… I thought that would hurt you.'

Her gaze flickered, her expression closing up and becoming for once unreadable. 'I should never have told you that, should I? Never have said I loved you. That was my mistake.'

A brief flare of remembered agony went through him once again, at the memory of the painful hope in her eyes that night, and the pressure of his own terrible longing. A longing for a life that would never be his. A life with her.

He crushed the memory. Pain was another flaw he had cut out of his life. 'It was not a mistake,' he said roughly. 'But it was why I sent that email, yes. I thought a clean break would be easier.'

She stared at him. 'Easier for who? For me or for yourself?'

'Sidonie…' he began.

But she suddenly got to her feet and put out a hand, her palm landing on his bare chest, a starburst of heat crackling over his skin. He lost his breath, every muscle he had gathering tight.

'I didn't just lose a friend, Khalil,' she said, looking up at him, searching his face. 'Don't you understand? That night you broke my heart.'

Pain twisted inside him, the flex of an agony he shouldn't feel. Hurting her had never been the goal, but of course he'd hurt her. She'd told him she loved him, she'd revealed her heart to him, a heart that had been trodden on and walked over for years by her aunt, and he'd just…walked away.

You cannot let that matter. You did what you had to do.

He had. The decision to leave her, to cut her off, had been the hardest of his life, but that was what he'd been brought up to do: to make the hard decisions. To make them so people like her didn't have to.

He did not regret that decision. He'd had to make it for both of their sakes. But…it was obvious that the wound he'd caused had been deeper than he'd thought. And it hadn't healed. He could see by the pain in her eyes.

Apologies were the sign of a weak ruler, his mother had always said. A king made his decisions and he stood by them. He didn't doubt and he certainly never admitted to his mistakes.

But this had hurt her, and he wanted to make it up to her, to make it right, and there was only one way he knew how to do that. Words got in the way, and he was tired of talking, so he put his hand over hers where it rested on his chest and then he pulled her into his arms.

CHAPTER SEVEN

SIDONIE HADN'T WANTED to admit to him how he'd hurt her. She'd sworn she wasn't going to allow him to get to under her skin the way he'd done years ago, because to admit to that pain was to admit that he still mattered to her, even now.

Except he did matter. The loss of the man who'd once been the most important person in her life mattered. She couldn't deny it, and as he'd stood there, telling her that man was gone, that friendship couldn't matter to a king, she hadn't been able to hold back.

She wanted him to know what his walking away from her, his cutting her off had done, that he'd broken her heart. And maybe it had been a mistake to reveal that to him, but she couldn't keep hiding her hurt, not any more. It was too hard.

The problem is you, no matter what he said. You should never have told him you loved him.

She shouldn't have, not after the lessons she'd learned in her aunt's house. When to ask for anything or to reveal any feeling at all, even her joy, was an unwanted intrusion. But that night in Soho, she'd wanted him to know. He'd signed her marriage promise and she'd thought… She'd thought he'd felt the same way. A mistake.

He'd told her it hadn't been, that he'd been trying to protect her because he'd had to go back to being a king, that he couldn't be her friend any longer, and she still didn't understand why. None of what he said about flaws and having to be more than a man made any sense.

But maybe that didn't matter right now.

It was all in the past and he was right here, his ink-black eyes looking down into hers, the hand at her back holding her firmly against him, making her aware of all the leashed power and strength contained in that muscled chest and ridged stomach, those powerful thighs…

She was aching deep inside, all the longing in her broken heart spilling out of her.

'I know, *ya hayati,*' he murmured and then raised both hands and cupped her face between them. Her heart was beating so loud she could barely hear him. 'And I will make it up to you, I promise.'

Then he tilted her head back and covered her mouth with his.

She sighed, intense relief sweeping through her. Despite her anger and sense of hurt, she'd been hoping for this moment, longing for it. And, while she'd had great plans of not letting her emotions get in the way once again, she couldn't remember what those plans were or even why she wanted to do that in the first place.

What was important now was that his mouth was on hers and he was kissing her, and all she wanted to do was melt into that kiss. To glory in it then give back to him all the pleasure that he was giving her.

She leaned into him and he angled her head back further, kissing her deeper, hungrier, and this time she began to kiss him back, tentative at first and then, as he made a soft growling sound in the back of his throat, with more confidence. He tasted so good, hot and rich and dark, like the very best chocolate and the finest brandy all rolled into one. She couldn't get enough.

His teeth sank into her bottom lip, giving her a nip that sent white-hot sparks of sensation along every single nerve ending, making her shudder in his arms. And then he was easing her down and onto the couch, his hands moving from her jaw to the neckline of her dress, pushing the golden fabric off her shoulders. The neckline was wide and loose anyway, so it didn't take much doing, and then she was sitting on the couch, bare to the waist.

The realisation sent a hot shock through her, but then he was bending over her, his mouth still on hers, her head resting on the back of the couch, kissing her senseless as his fingers brushed down the side of her neck to her collarbones, stroking gently. Then moving further down, delicately tracing the curve of one bare breast, touching her as if she was made of glass and had to be handled with care.

Her nipples tightened and she shivered, part of her reeling that this was actually happening, that she was half naked and he was touching her, while another part wanted more and harder and right now, because she was going to go up in flames and she didn't want to just yet…not quite yet.

She had waited for him for so long. She couldn't bear to wait any more.

'Khal…' she whispered against his mouth, arching into his hand. 'Khal, please…'

But he only gentled the kiss, turning it into a slow, deep exploration, at the same time as his fingers kept on brushing over her curves, learning her, stroking her skin as if he couldn't get enough of the feel of it.

She shuddered, her breath coming faster, ripples of delight forming wherever his fingers touched and moving outward, increasing that dragging, aching pressure that was concentrated between her thighs.

He circled one nipple lazily, tracing small circles around and around, teasing her, making her shudder and twist on the cushions, and then, just when she thought she was going to go mad, his thumb brushed over the tip of her breast, sending an arrow of such intense pleasure through her that she gasped aloud. Then he did it again, and again, and she gasped a second time, reaching for his hand to guide it where she wanted it.

'No.' His lips brushed hers as he moved his thumb back and forth over her nipple. 'Keep still for me, *ya hayati*. I will give you what you want, but I am going to savour this first. I am going to savour you.'

'But I... I...don't mind,' she said breathlessly. 'I want—'

'I know what you want.' His voice was very deep and very certain. 'But I have waited years for you and so I am going to take my time. You deserve nothing less.'

Years. He'd been waiting years.

Her heart squeezed tight in her chest. There were so many things she wanted to say that right now she didn't care about what she deserved, she only wanted him to end this exquisite torment, but it was clear that nothing she could do was going to stop him.

So she let her hand fall away and kept still as he kissed her long and deep and lazy, his hand stroking one breast and then the other, making her pant and arch, the pressure between her thighs becoming almost unbearable.

The way he touched her made her ache, made her feel vulnerable, made her remember all those fleeting moments of contact over the years. The gentle hand on her arm, the touch on her shoulder. The warmth of his arms as he'd pulled her in for that dance the night of her birthday. No one had ever held her the way he had. No one had ever touched her the way he did. No one had ever touched her full stop. Not since her parents had died. Her aunt hadn't hugged her, or kissed her, had never even laid a hand on her shoulder for comfort, not even at her parents' funeral. She hadn't realised how starved for touch she'd been until now.

Until Khalil's stroking her, caressing her as if she

was a work of art he needed to be careful with. A precious work of art.

Had she ever felt precious to anyone? No, she didn't think she had, but she felt it now. She felt precious to him.

He put one knee on the cushion beside her, his powerful body leaning further over her, his mouth moving down her neck to the hollow of her throat and lingering, tasting the frantic beat of her pulse. His palm was hot against one breast and he squeezed it gently, making her shudder, then he slid it down further, beneath the gold fabric of her dress, over her stomach.

Sidonie went utterly still, every part of her trembling as his fingers slid lower. She let her thighs fall open, desperate for him to touch her there, and he finally did, pushing beneath the waistband of the lacy knickers she wore and brushing over the slick folds of her sex.

She cried out, lifting her hips into his hand, wanting more, but he only stroked her lazily, his fingers sliding and exploring everywhere except the place where she needed it most. His mouth lingered at her throat and then moved lower, tasting the curve of one breast. Then his tongue traced a burning circle around her nipple, his fingers between her thighs mirroring the movement, again and again, until she was whispering his name, barely conscious of what she was saying.

Then right when she thought she couldn't bear another second, the heat of his mouth closed over her aching nipple at the same time as his fingers moved between her thighs, brushing over the most sensitive part of her, and the pressure inside her burst apart like a firework, the most intense, unbearable, incredible pleasure flooding through her.

She gave a helpless cry of ecstasy, shaking and shaking and unable to stop, until she thought she might come apart at the seams. But then he was on the couch beside her, pulling her into his lap, his arms warm and strong around her, holding her, keeping her together as the aftershocks passed.

She lay against him, her head on his shoulder, relaxed and heavy and sated, unable to move and not wanting to either.

He was very still and gradually she became conscious that, though the beat of his heart was strong and steady, all his muscles were tense. She could feel the hard press of his arousal and it made her flush with heat. That was because of her, wasn't it? She'd aroused him, she'd made him hard. That was all her.

She shifted her head on his shoulder and looked up at him. He was staring back, his eyes sharp as shattered obsidian, a deep, hot glitter in them.

'Khal,' she said huskily. 'Do you need—?'

'No.' There was an unfamiliar, rough edge to his voice. 'That was for you and only for you. You do not have to reciprocate.'

'But you're hard.'

He lifted one eyebrow. 'So? I am quite able to manage myself, believe me.'

She swallowed, searching his face, something inside her falling away. And the question came out before she could stop herself. 'Is it me?'

He frowned. 'What do you mean?'

'You're hard but you don't want me to touch you. You don't want me to give you pleasure.' Her chest felt tight, an echo of his rejection from so long ago resounding through her. 'Is there something the matter with me? Is that why you don't—?'

Khalil laid a finger across her mouth, silencing her, a burning look in his eyes. 'There is nothing wrong with you, Sidonie. *Nothing*. Why would you say that?'

She shook his finger away, her heart beating far too fast. Protecting herself was instinctive these days, but there was no protecting herself from him. She understood that now. 'Why wouldn't I think that? All I got from Aunt May was how much of a burden I was and how grateful I should be for every little thing she gave me. She made me ask for everything, and I always felt so needy and desperate when I did. And then...' Her throat was tight, and she had to swallow past the lump in it. 'When you walked away from me that night, I thought I'd frightened you away. I thought that Aunt May was right about me. I *was* too needy and desperate. I was just... wrong somehow.'

The words hung in the air between them, and she wished abruptly that she could take them back. She'd been too honest and that left her vulnerable.

She shivered, but didn't look away, even though

part of her was dreading his response. She wouldn't be a coward.

His gaze was full of darkness, but something bright glowed at the heart of it, a flame that burned hot and strong. 'It is a good thing your aunt is in England. If she was here, I would have had her imprisoned.' A note of ferocity vibrated in his voice. 'And I would have had myself thrown into a cell with her.'

Sidonie took a shaky breath. 'The problem isn't you. The problem is—'

'The problem is that your aunt stifled and starved you,' he interrupted harshly. 'She hurt you. The way she brought you up was a crime, and the fact that despite that you remain such a warm, bright light is a testament to your strength and your courage.'

She blinked, staring at him, her heart squeezing tighter and tighter.

'And I did not help,' he went on. 'I did not think about how leaving you would affect you. I knew cutting you off completely would hurt you, but I thought that you would heal.' His arms around her tightened, the look in his eyes abruptly intensifying. 'You asked me whether it was easier for you or for myself, and the truth is… The truth is that it was for myself. Because I did not want to leave you, *ya hayati*. I wanted to stay with you. I wanted to give you the family you wanted and be at your side. I wanted to marry you. But my country needed me. I could not have that longing in my heart and still be a king.'

'Khalil,' she whispered, her throat tight and sore.

'No, I have not finished. You wondered where your friend is? He died, Sidonie. Leaving you hurt him, and because I could not have that pain and be the king my country needed me to be, I had to destroy him.'

Her heart was now a hot, sharp ball in her chest, full of jagged edges. He was telling the truth, she could hear it in the intense note in his voice, in that flame in his eyes. It made her throat close with bittersweet anguish, and an old, remembered grief.

The look on his face that night as she'd told him she loved him, his expression becoming hard and cold and set. A stranger's face.

This man's face. The King's face.

But inside he hadn't been hard and cold. He hadn't wanted to go. He'd wanted to stay with her.

There were tears in her eyes now; she couldn't stop them. And she didn't know what to say. He'd told her that the friend she knew was gone, that he'd destroyed him. But part of her didn't believe that. Because if that was true, why had he told her all of this? Why had he come back to England? Why had he been so insistent on marrying her?

Oh, he'd had many reasons and they all sounded good, but... His mouth on hers had been so hot and hungry, and she'd been able to taste his need. His desperation.

He'd brought her here for a reason, and maybe he wasn't fully aware of what the real reason was, but she knew.

He'd brought her here to save him.

She lifted her hand and touched his face. 'I don't think he's dead, Khal. I think he's still here. And I think he needs me.'

Sidonie's pretty face was flushed and those fascinating emerald-green eyes of hers held a softness he remembered. It was painful, that softness, reminding him of too many things he didn't want to recall.

But he didn't want to let her go, no matter how painful or otherwise it was to have her there.

Giving her pleasure had tested both his control and his patience to the limit. She had blushed so beautifully, had whispered his name so huskily, and her skin had felt like satin and had tasted as sweet as he'd thought it would—no, it had tasted better. Made him hungry for more, to have her naked with nothing between them.

But this wasn't about him and what he wanted. This was about her and wanting to give her pleasure to make up for all the years of pain, and he had. He just hadn't expected her to turn around and want to give him the same back again.

You should have. She was never one just to take.

Of course she wasn't. But he'd needed time to get himself under control. He'd felt too close to the edge, and she called that old poisonous blood to the surface far too easily.

Except then she'd taken his refusal as a rejection and there had been pain in her eyes. Pain in her voice as she'd talked about her aunt. And some part of him hadn't been able to let that go.

He should have known it would all lead back to Aunt May and her emotionally barren upbringing, and he just couldn't let her believe that there was something needy and desperate about her. As if those things were wrong, which they weren't. Sidonie had lost her parents too young and had been brought up by someone who'd withheld the love and affection she should have had.

That didn't make her needy and desperate. It made her hungry because she'd been starved.

Knowing that meant he couldn't hold back the truth about what had happened all those years ago. She should know how desperately he'd wanted to stay with her and how leaving her had caused him pain. Because it had. And how he'd had to cut away that part of himself. A king could not be broken. A king was strength enduring and there could be no flaws, no jagged pieces of a shattered friendship piercing his heart.

There were no flaws in him now, so he wasn't sure why her soft words sent a jolt of electricity down his spine. She was wrong, of course. The dead part of him was gone.

He took her hand from his cheekbone, kissed her fingertips. 'If he were still alive, *ya hayati*, he would. But he is not. Come, we did not have our dinner in Paris, and I do not want to deny you the birthday feast I promised.'

Yet she didn't move, her red hair over his shoulder as she looked up at him, her gaze glinting green from beneath long, auburn lashes. 'I don't think you brought me here for your country, Khal,' she murmured. 'I think you told yourself that and I think you believe that. But that's not really the reason, is it?'

He stilled. That gaze of hers, it seemed to see inside him. The way it had years ago. She'd always seen deeper than other people. Everyone at Oxford had thought his arrogance had been a pride thing—even Galen and Augustine. But only she had understood that it had been a self-protective thing, to keep people at a distance. He'd never told her why, had only said that Yusuf had been injured in the succession battle, because he couldn't bear to tell her the truth, that he'd killed him. He couldn't tell her either, about the shadow Yusuf's death had cast over his life, or about the doubts that had plagued him. Doubts the heir to the throne should never have had.

He hadn't wanted to tarnish her light with his darkness.

He couldn't even bear to do it now.

She's right, though, you did bring her here for you.

No. She was here for his people, his court. For his country. He wanted to marry her for them, not for himself. He wanted her, it was true, but that was a purely physical want. A man had needs certainly, but he wasn't a man, not any more. He was a king.

'There is no deeper reason, Sidonie,' he said, an edge creeping into his voice. 'What I told you about being the queen my people need is true.'

'Maybe. But why care about me, then?' She pulled her hand from his and touched his cheek again, her fingers light and cool against his skin. 'Why give me these beautiful dresses and prepare dinners for me? Why give me two weeks? Why agree to be the patron of my charity? Why bother to discuss this with me at all?'

Everything in him tightened. 'Because I wanted your agreement. I did not want to demand or use force. Those are my father's tactics, and I will not use them.'

'No, Khal.' Her hand dropped to his chest, her fingers trailing over his skin, stroking him. 'You can tell yourself those things, but I don't think they're true.' Her gaze was so clear, so direct. 'I think I'm here because my friend needs me and I'm the only one who can save him.'

'I have told you, that is not—'

But this time it was her turn to silence him with a gentle finger across his mouth. 'You don't have to be a king with me, Khalil. You never did. Just as you were never a prince all those years ago.' She lifted the finger then dropped her hand over the front of his trousers, tracing his rapidly hardening length through the fabric. 'You were just a man back then, just my friend. And you can be that now, don't you see? You don't have to be anything more than who you already are with me.'

His whole body felt tight, the heat inside him building. And he wanted to stop her, because his body, after all, was only a man's and it was tired of constant control. It wanted her. It had been waiting for her for ten years and it didn't want to wait any more.

Yet what she was saying couldn't be. That man had known happiness, had known love, but it wasn't something that was possible for a king. A king was a surgeon, cutting out anything that might make his country sick, and sometimes that was healthy tissue. He needed steady hands for it, and a cold, clear, analytical brain. He couldn't afford to be at the mercy of either his body or his heart.

Except he could feel need inside him, that desperate, terrible longing he thought he'd excised so long ago. The longing for her. For her hands and her mouth, and the beautiful body he'd fantasised about and wanted so badly. For her heat to chase away the dark.

He could have that at least, couldn't he? It was only physical, and after all, he was going to need heirs at some point. No, she hadn't agreed yet to marry him, but perhaps if he gave her what she wanted now, she might.

He could remember what it was like to be that man for her. Not pretend—he had no need to fake anything with her—but he could try to be at least a little like that man again. He couldn't be him totally, but maybe with her alone he could.

He'd just have to make sure when he was away from her to be the King he had to be.

Her hand pressed against him, the heat of her palm seeping through the light cotton of his trousers. The breath hissed in his throat, a spike of pure pleasure lancing through him.

Her eyes had darkened, and so he put his own hand over hers and held it against him, the light pressure almost agonising.

Her fingers squeezed lightly.

'Sidonie…' Her name came out half a groan, half a growl.

She moved closer, her scent all around him, her warmth seductive as a siren's song, making him acutely aware of every second of those ten years of longing.

'I want you, Khalil,' she said huskily, the honesty that was at the core of her laid bare. 'I want to give you pleasure.' Her eyes had darkened still further, like shadowed forests. 'Teach me. Teach me how to make you feel good. Please…' The way she said the words, the plea in her voice…

Desire burned hot in his blood, the way she was touching him making it difficult to think. Not that there was any thinking needed. Not when he'd already made his decision.

Khalil pulled her hand away and lay back on the couch cushions with her on top of him, her soft warmth against his chest. She was very flushed, the slightest hint of challenge in her eyes. A shudder of heat coursed down his spine, his heartbeat accelerating.

'You wanted to touch me,' he said roughly. 'So touch me like this.' And he took her hand and drew it down over his stomach, to the waistband of his trousers, then beneath the loose linen fabric and under the cotton of his underwear, to where he was hard and ready for her.

Her eyes widened, her mouth opening slightly as he curled her fingers around him. A sigh escaped her.

'Yes,' he growled, the pressure of her hand sweet agony. 'Stroke me, Sidonie.'

So she did. Hesitantly at first, then with growing confidence, her gaze on his, watching his reaction to her touch.

It was incredibly erotic. But he wanted to taste her so he reached out and slid a hand behind the back of her head, pulling her mouth down on his, kissing her hungrily.

Sidonie moaned and kissed him back, her hand moving, doing what he told her to and stroking him.

The intensity of the pleasure was impossible to contain. Every nerve-ending he had was alight from the touch of her hand and the taste of her mouth. He'd waited years for her touch. Years and years. Had once wanted it more than life itself.

He had it now and it was going to destroy him.

Well, he would let it. Because in this moment, she was right. He didn't have to be a king. Right now, with her, he could be a man, take all the pleasure and passion she was giving him and drown himself in it.

So for the first time in his life, Khalil didn't think. He didn't reflect or pause to examine the implications. He acted on instinct, driven by desire and desperation, and a need deeper than words.

He shifted, pulling her hand away from him and

turning her over onto her back, settling himself between her thighs. Then he bent and kissed her again, hungrier than he'd ever been in his entire life. 'I have to have you, Sidonie,' he said in a voice he didn't recognise as his own. 'I have to have you, *now.*'

CHAPTER EIGHT

THE WORDS WERE rough gravel and velvet and the heat in them nearly set her alight. He was a hot, heavy weight on her, pressing her into the couch cushions, and she loved it. She loved the feel of him pinning her there, holding her down, reducing her world to the softness of the cushions beneath her, and the hardness of the man on top of her.

'Yes,' she whispered, her hands sliding up his chest, pushing the robe he was wearing off his powerful shoulders, wanting to keep on touching him because the feel of his skin, velvety smooth and so hot, was like a drug she couldn't get enough of. 'Oh, yes. *Please.*'

She thought she'd got through to him and that some part of him had heard her. He'd resisted her telling him the man was still a part of him, his body taut with negation, but something in him had surrendered to her.

Now it was her turn to surrender to him.

It was as if something had been unleashed inside him, because his mouth was on hers again and he was kissing her deeply, with all the intensity that was part of him. And Sidonie felt herself go up in flames.

There was nothing in the entire world except the heat of his mouth and his skin beneath her fingers, the wild, intoxicating taste of him and his hands pulling at her dress, easing it up, getting it out of the way. Then he tugged at her underwear, the flimsy lace of her knickers tearing and coming away so she was naked from the waist down.

He freed himself from his loose trousers and underwear, and then he was right there, between her thighs, pushing inside her. She gasped, feeling herself stretch around him. It burned, but she was so ready for him that the burning sensation stopped almost as soon as it had begun. There was no pain as he pushed deeper, only an intense feeling of fullness that had her shifting and squirming beneath him, trying to find some space for herself, because it felt as if he took up every part of her.

Then he slid one hand behind her right knee, lifting her leg up and over his hip, opening her up so he could ease deeper, making her gasp aloud, shuddering as the sense of fullness became more intense.

'Sidonie,' he murmured, his deep voice rough and full of heat. 'My Sidonie...' He looked down at her, his gaze black and velvety and all-encompassing. 'You are mine, *ya hayati*.' The fierce, possessive note in the words thrilled her down to the bone. 'You know it. You feel it.'

He began to move inside her, flexing his hips in a deep thrust in before a slow, delicious slide out, turning the sensation from an uncomfortable fullness to an insistent, aching pleasure that tore a moan from her throat.

She couldn't look away, pinned to the couch as much by the look in his eyes as by the thrust of his hips, and soon she was moving with him, watching the same pleasure she felt burning in her light the darkness of his eyes.

She did feel it. Because this was what he'd always given her, the release of the passion inside her, all the deep feelings living with her aunt had stifled.

Yet it hadn't been her aunt stifling her these past five years. It had been herself. She'd protected her heart, saved it from pain, and yet as he moved inside her, the pleasure intensifying, she knew she'd lost something.

Something he was giving back to her, right here in this moment.

His name escaped like a prayer as ecstasy began to overtake her, and her nails dug into his shoulders because it was too much and yet not enough.

He'd always been giving her things. Birthday presents and parties. The rare treasure of his smile. The gift of his anger at those who hurt her, and the most important thing of all: acceptance.

He'd accepted the wild part of her, the passionate part. The part she'd locked away for years after her aunt had crushed it and he'd given her the key to unlock it again. And he'd gloried in it as much as she had.

'Don't stop.' The words fell helplessly from her,

and she let them. Just as she let him see what he was doing to her. 'Please, Khal. Please don't stop.'

He didn't say anything, but his gaze flared and he moved faster, harder. He slid one hand behind her head, holding her still, and then he bent and covered her mouth once again in a kiss so hot it felt like a brand against her skin.

Her heart swelled inside her, pushing painfully against her ribs.

He still gloried in that part of her. She'd pushed back at him, but he hadn't taken her 'no' for an answer. He hadn't let her push him away. And now she was here with him above her, inside her, all around her, wanting her, demanding her passion...

She couldn't hold herself back any longer.

She surrendered, losing herself to the pleasure he was giving her, the pleasure they were creating together, building like a bonfire, adding more tinder until it was a roaring conflagration, blazing into the night.

Then just before the orgasm hit her, catapulting her into the stratosphere, she knew with a bone-deep certainty that, whatever she'd told herself about leaving in two weeks, it was lie.

She'd come back with him because she wanted him. Because she'd wanted *this*. She'd always wanted it. And she'd never stopped wanting, not deep down in the depths of her heart.

Because she'd loved him then and she loved him now. She'd never stopped loving him.

The knowledge was intrinsic and cell-deep, then

it was lost in the storm as the pleasure overwhelmed her. And all she was aware of was the hard thrust of Khalil's hips and then his deep voice growling her name as it took him, too.

For a time afterwards there was stillness and silence, broken only by the sound of their breathing, rough and ragged. He didn't move, his body a heavy weight that she was in no hurry to escape. In fact, she never wanted to escape it.

And you don't have to. Not if you marry him.

The thought made tears start in her eyes and her throat close. She couldn't tell herself now she didn't want this with her whole heart.

She still loved him. Of course she'd marry him. He'd said something about kings not being permitted love, but what did that matter? If she was his wife, he'd never be able to walk away from her again.

He shifted, easing his weight from her, lifting his head, and looking down at her. His gaze, normally as unreadable as a shard of obsidian, was full of emotional currents and she stared back, trying to read him.

'What is it?' she asked, lifting a hand to his face, hungry for the feel of his skin.

'I did not intend to take you like an animal on the couch,' he said after a moment. 'It was not supposed to happen like that.'

She smiled. 'But I like you being an animal.'

He didn't smile back, a fierce gleam in his eyes. 'You were a virgin. Do not think I did not notice.'

Oh, that. She'd forgotten about that. She was glad

she'd waited for him, though. Not that she'd waited, she knew now. It was either him or no one.

'Does it matter?' she asked.

'I would not have been so...demanding if I had known.'

She let her fingertips brush over the sharp line of his jaw, the light prickle of his stubble against her skin. 'I want you to be demanding. In fact, I demand that you be demanding.'

Something in his face relaxed, and for the first time since he'd come back into her life the dark shadows in his gaze lightened. 'Did you wait for me, *ya hayati*?'

'Of course.' There was no reason to hide the truth from him. 'You said I was yours, and I am. Just as you've always been mine.'

He turned his face into her hand, his mouth brushing her palm. 'In that case, I cannot help but notice that you have given yourself to me.'

'Yes? And?'

His gaze shifted, turning hot. 'That means I am your husband already in everything but name.'

A hot, electric feeling pulsed through her. He'd always been intense, but this was intensity on a whole other level. Certainty blazed in his eyes, along with a possessiveness he'd never turned on her before. It made every part of her ache. Her aunt had never cared about her. Her aunt had never wanted her. But Khalil... He was looking at her as if he'd been searching half his life for her, and was now determined not to let her out of his sight.

'Hmm,' she murmured, tracing the line of his lower lip, deciding he could bear a little teasing. 'Are you wanting to renegotiate the two weeks you gave me?'

'No.' He nipped at her fingertips, an unfamiliar wickedness now in his gaze. 'I am wanting to dispense with it completely.'

Her heart turned over in her chest. The look on his face, intense and yet with a slight playfulness, reminded her of the old Khal. Of him when he wanted his way and would try and convince her with humour.

He's still in there. He's still him.

'A new agreement, then?' She kept her tone light while her heart thudded hard in her ears.

'A new agreement,' he confirmed. 'You belong in my bed and at my side, *ya hayati*. You always have. And I do not think you want to wait two weeks to decide. I think you already know what you want now.'

She did. But he could work for it. 'Oh? I do?'

'Yes.' The edge of his teeth grazed her fingertips again, making her shiver. 'You want to be my wife.'

He was so arrogant she wanted to laugh, the way she had years ago. 'And I suppose you're going to insist, are you?' She was smiling; she couldn't help herself.

'I am.' Abruptly, the playfulness died out of his eyes, leaving behind only intensity. 'I told you that my country needed you, Sidonie. And they do. But… you were right. I need you, too. And… I want this.

I want you.' He paused. 'I do not beg for anything. But I will beg for you if you require it.'

Her heart squeezed tight. He would. She could see it in his eyes.

She wanted to tell him right there and then that he didn't need to, that she'd marry him because she loved him, but those were words she couldn't say quite yet. They'd driven him away the last time and she wasn't sure what he'd think of them now.

'Love, friendship...they are not allowed for a king.'

Well, she could wait. Perhaps later, as his wife, she could convince him otherwise.

'That,' she said, 'is the most romantic proposal I've ever heard.'

He shifted, his body once more settling on hers, pinning her. His hard mouth curved, and she could see amusement in his eyes. 'It is not a proposal. It is an order.'

She laughed, lifting her hands to take his beautiful face between them. You don't have to order me to be your wife, Khal.'

'Sidonie, I—'

'Yes, I will marry you. Yes, I will be your queen.'

A blaze of heat and triumph lit his eyes. 'Then I will—'

'On one condition.'

His gaze narrowed. 'What condition?'

It was something she'd thought of just now, because of course being his wife would have implications for her charity. Excellent implications.

'You are still to be the patron of my charity. And I will not be giving it up, understand? In fact, being your queen will open up a lot of opportunities for us. So, you'll have to provide me with everything I need to run it remotely. Plus, I'll need to visit England regularly in order to keep an eye on things.'

This time his smile was slow and utterly heart-melting, easing the tense lines of his face, lighting up the darkness in his eyes. A smile of pleasure and such warmth that her heart tightened in recognition.

It was him. It was her Khal.

'You drive a hard bargain, *ya hayati*. But yes, I think I can accommodate those conditions. But I, too, have some of my own.'

She stroked the line of his jaw, loving the velvety feel of his skin. 'Oh?'

Khalil gripped her wrists gently. 'I need you in my bed. Every night from now on.'

Sidonie pretended to think about it for, oh, half a second. 'Okay. Yes. I want that too.'

'Good. In that case we will be married tomorrow.'

An electric shock arrowed down her spine. 'Tomorrow?'

Khalil eased her hands away, pressing them down on either side of her head. 'Yes, my Sidonie. Tomorrow. I have already waited five years and I am tired of it.'

She didn't resist, conscious that beneath her shock there was also excitement and a gathering anticipation. 'But isn't that too soon to organise anything?'

'No. Not if I will it. I am the King.' He gave her

the most ridiculously smug look she'd ever seen. 'In a month we will have a grand celebration of our marriage and you will be formally crowned, but my people have already observed me carrying you from the plane. They know you are my intended. Some may be unhappy with the speed and wish for more ceremony, but once you are legally my wife there will be no disagreements or protests. I will make sure of it.'

He was so certain, so absolutely sure of himself. Sometimes that certainty of his drove her crazy and sometimes it was the most reassuring thing in the entire world.

She found it reassuring now.

'Okay,' she said huskily. 'Then tomorrow it is.'

The intense, possessive look was back in his eyes. 'And now, *ya hayati,* I suggest we start practising for our wedding night.'

'Good,' she said happily. 'I thought you'd never ask.' Then she lifted her head and kissed his beautiful mouth and lost herself for the rest of the night.

Much later, after the remains of a very late dinner had been cleared away and Sidonie was where she should have been years ago, fast asleep in his bed, Khalil stepped out of the French doors and into his private courtyard.

He felt too energised to sleep, as if something that had been wrong for many years was now suddenly right, that pressure inside him abruptly lifted.

Finally, after so long, she would be his wife.

He hadn't realised, not fully, what making love

to her would mean to him. Or perhaps some part of him had known, but he hadn't wanted to admit it to himself.

The moment he'd pushed inside her and felt her around him, holding him tight, and he'd stared down into her green eyes, seeing her…seeing *her,* all sunshine and sweetness and warmth. And she'd looked back, her face so beautifully flushed, the pleasure they'd created between them glowing in her eyes…

Perhaps she'd been right, he'd thought. That he *had* brought her here for him, to save some part of him he'd thought lost for ever. It felt wrong to think it though, because that was an indulgence, something his father might have done. Putting his own selfish greed before the needs of his nation.

Yet finally being inside her there on the couch… it had felt so right. As if that had been where he'd always meant to end up, as if she was his destiny somehow. The rush of possessiveness that had then followed had shocked him, and he hadn't been able to hold it back.

He couldn't let her go. He couldn't. Yes, she was for his country, but having a wife he wanted would be good for him. A wife he trusted. A wife he'd enjoy getting heirs with.

A wife who knows you, deep down.

Yes, she knew him. Knew parts of him, the man he'd been certainly. But she didn't know everything. She didn't know what he'd had to do to make himself strong, the lessons his mother had taught him to protect him.

Hard lessons.

He couldn't tell her about them, though. She didn't need to hear how painful they'd been. It was his own pain, and he would be the caretaker of it.

But the most important thing was that she'd agreed to be his wife. Now she would help him change his kingdom for the better. She would help him rebuild what his father had broken. And he would help her in turn with her charity. He'd rip out the substandard office in the Queens' wing and install the fastest internet connection he could, ensure that she had all the technology she needed. Perhaps he'd even buy her a royal jet of her own so she could come and go to England as she pleased.

They'd discussed it over dinner and then she'd filled him in on the progress she'd made over the past five years. He'd been so impressed. Her charity work was amazing, and she had such vision. Such drive. She'd always had that, even back in university.

Satisfaction filled him. She was going to make the most remarkable Queen.

Tomorrow couldn't come soon enough.

At that moment his phone buzzed and he took it out of his pocket, glancing down at the screen, then hitting the answer button. 'Galen.'

'Khal. You left me a message. Is this about our meeting next month in Al Da'ira?'

Every month, or whenever their schedules allowed it, he, Galen, and Augustine would get together to renew their friendship and to allow themselves time to be just men, not kings. Also to remember old times, when they'd been the 'Wicked Princes' back at Oxford, causing mayhem in their respective colleges and breaking hearts everywhere.

One of the three would usually host their get-togethers and it was Khalil's turn next month. He'd already decided ages ago that the timing would be perfect to host an engagement ball just like the one Galen had had for his beautiful wife, Solace. His friends already knew of Sidonie—they'd teased him good-naturedly back at university about their friendship—but Khalil had made sure to keep her away from them, since both Galen and Augustine had been unrepentant playboys and Sidonie was nothing if not lovely. Galen, however, was now happily married, though Augustine had remained the same unrepentant playboy as he'd been all those years ago.

However, now it would not be an engagement ball.

'Yes,' he said. 'I wish to throw a celebration for my marriage while you and Augustine are here, and I could use your advice.'

There was a long silence down the other end of the phone and then a strange choking sound.

Khalil stared at the fountain in his courtyard and frowned. 'Galen? Are you still there?'

'Yes.' His friend sounded slightly strangled. 'A celebration for your marriage? When did this happen?'

'It has not happened. Not yet. I am getting married tomorrow.'

Galen coughed. 'You've been keeping that quiet.'

'Keeping what quiet?'

'The fact that you even had a fiancée.'

'You did not need to know,' he said, since it was the truth.

'You are, as ever, an enigma, Khal.' Galen sounded amused. 'So are you going to tell me who the lucky woman is, or do I have to guess?'

'You remember Sidonie? My friend at Oxford? Her.'

There was another long silence and then Galen laughed. 'Oh, yes, I remember. Very quiet and studious. Pretty, though, which was why you kept us away from her, I seem to recall.'

Khalil scowled as a wave of possessive annoyance filled him. 'I fail to see what is amusing about it.'

'Nothing is amusing,' Galen said soothingly. 'It's only that you were quite certain about the fact that she was only a friend.'

'She is only a friend. But she will also be my wife. The two are not mutually exclusive.'

'I see.' Galen's tone was very neutral. 'So you are not in love with her, then?'

Electricity prickled through him. Perhaps he *had* been in love with her back then, not that he'd ever told his friends about it. She'd certainly loved him. But love, along with all the rest of those very human emotions, was forbidden to a king and so he'd cut it out of his life.

He certainly wasn't in love with her any more.

'This has nothing to do with love, Galen,' he said curtly. 'I chose her because she is just what my court and my country needs. I will explain when you get here.'

Again, there was a silence.

Galen had changed since he'd met his wife, Solace, becoming much more relaxed and open. He ruled with a lighter touch than he once had and Khalil was sure it had something to do with his beautiful wife.

He was in love, he'd told Khalil and Augustine when they'd commented on his good mood, and, while Khalil had been pleased for him, love wasn't anything he could allow himself.

'I look forward to it,' Galen said, still sounding suspiciously neutral. 'So tell me, what kind of celebration are you thinking?'

Khalil gave him a few thoughts, and five minutes later the call ended with Galen promising to get his events team—which was far better than Khalil's own—in contact with some of Khalil's staff so they could start planning.

After that, Khalil pulled up Augustine's number because his other friend needed to know and he should hear it from Khalil personally.

'Khal,' Augustine answered in his rich, melted-honey voice. 'It's been a while. How are things at home?'

Unlike Khalil's own reign, Augustine's had been calm and relatively untroubled. His father had been a good king, and Augustine looked to be carrying on the tradition. He'd mentioned once to Galen and Khalil that he'd been thinking of abdicating, though he refused to tell them why. But he hadn't abdicated yet, and Khalil was starting to wonder if it was all just a bluff.

'Fine,' Khalil said. 'I assume you're coming next month?'

'But of course.' Augustine sounded amused for some reason. Then again, Augustine always sounded as if he was enjoying some kind of private joke that no one else was privy to. 'Wild horses couldn't keep me away.'

'Good. Because I will be throwing a ball to celebrate my marriage.'

'Your marriage?' Augustine sounded surprised, as well he might. 'When did this happen? Has Galen been putting ideas into your head?'

'It will be happening tomorrow,' Khalil said. 'And no, it is not Galen. It is merely time. My country needs a queen and I need heirs.'

'Ah, heirs,' Augustine drawled. 'That old chestnut. Well, better you than me. So, do I know your fiancée? Or perhaps a better question: is she someone I've slept with? Could be awkward if so.'

It was a joke and Khalil treated it the way he treated all Augustine's jokes. He ignored it. 'It is Sidonie. Do you remember her? We were friends years ago at Oxford.'

'Her? Really?' More surprise echoed in his friend's voice.

And Khalil found he had the same response to Augustine that he'd had to Galen. 'Why is that so surprising?' he enquired, his tone dangerously soft.

'Only because I thought you'd have claimed her years ago.'

You should have. Instead, you broke her heart and left her for five years.

That ache, that flaw in what could surely not be his heart, throbbed.

He ignored it. 'And I was not going to,' he said stiffly. 'My situation has changed, however.'

'Has it? You took your time.'

A lecture from Sidonie was one thing. A lecture from Augustine was quite another.

'I did not ask for—'

'Or did she refuse you?'

Khalil's jaw went tight with unexpected temper. He didn't want to get into the particulars of what had happened with Sidonie, especially given how poorly he'd treated her. 'The ball will be—'

'Oh, so she did,' Augustine interrupted a second time, more amusement in his voice. 'What happened? Were you not convincing enough?'

'She has not refused.' Khalil held on to his temper but only just. 'She has accepted my proposal.'

'Just as well,' Augustine said. 'I was just going to suggest taking her to bed. She'll be begging for your ring by morning.'

'Why do women like you?' Khalil asked acidly. 'I cannot understand it.'

Augustine laughed, unoffended. 'My reputation is somewhat intriguing, I believe. And I live up to it. So tell me, is it love, Khal? Did you catch that nonsense from Galen?'

Again that electricity passed through him, as if the word was a badly earthed wire that he kept putting his hand on.

He didn't want to keep thinking about it.

'No,' he said flatly.

But doesn't she deserve to be loved?

Of course she did. She did more than anyone else he'd ever known. Except he couldn't give her that love. He never would.

'Thank God for that,' Augustine said. 'At least one of us is keeping his head. Well, I shall look forward to seeing her again.'

After he'd finished the call, Khalil took a couple of steps into the warm night of the courtyard, the fountain in the middle playing its gentle music. He had a million other things he wanted to think about, yet he couldn't stop thinking about Sidonie and the question of love.

It was true, he *had* loved her. He'd come to Oxford a dark and tormented man, and she'd truly been the sunshine in his life. Giving him back hope and the kind of happiness he'd only ever known as a very young boy, and maybe not even then.

She'd been his first love. Yet he'd never been able to forget that eventually he'd have to give her up. That he'd have to cut his heart out of his chest and sacrifice it for the good of his country. And indeed, that was what he'd done.

He could not love her again. Love—any of those warmer, softer emotions—was not allowed for kings, and especially not for a son of Amir.

Amir hadn't been the divine being his people had wanted. He'd been a petty, flawed man, and if Khalil wanted to be better, to be stronger than Amir, he had to be more than that. Being a true king of Al Da'ira meant not falling prey to the same greed that had tainted his father. The need for more wealth, more power, more physical indulgence.

His mother had told him it would always be harder for him than for other people because of that poisonous blood, so he had to be more careful. But he hadn't been careful in England. With Sidonie he'd always wanted more. More of her laughter, more of her empathy, more of her warmth. More of *her*.

He'd been greedy. That was the truth of why he'd had to leave her in the end.

And that was why love could never be a part of their relationship, no matter that she deserved it. He had to guard himself. He couldn't love her and be a king—the two were mutually exclusive for someone like him. Nor could he give up his country for her, not when he'd fought to the death for the right to rule. That would negate everything he'd done.

Khalil put his hands on the edge of the fountain and leaned on them, staring down into the water, unseeing.

A king wasn't supposed to care about individuals, only the wellbeing of his country as a whole, but he couldn't deny that he did care about Sidonie.

He cared that she'd lost her parents so young and had been brought up by her sorry excuse for an aunt.

He cared that he'd broken her heart all those years ago, and that heart of hers was still broken even now.

He wanted her to be happy, here with him.

It was dangerous, that caring. It was a flaw.

'Things are different for kings,' his mother had told him as she'd handed him the knife. *'They have to do hard things. They cannot be soft or uncertain, and they cannot let their emotions rule them. Especially you, Khalil. You have your father's blood and so you must be extra-careful.'*

He hadn't wanted that knife. He'd cried as she'd forced it into his hand, loathing the heavy weight of it in his palm, knowing even then what she wanted him to do. But his tears had made no impact. She'd been relentless, nodding to the servant to bring Dusk, his half-grown chocolate Labrador, into the room. The dog had started to get sick a week earlier, and even though the vet had done all he could to save him, it was clear that Dusk wasn't going to get better.

'You know what you need to do, Khalil,' his mother had said. *'Dusk will die in agony if you do not do this. And it must be you. He is your dog, and you are responsible for him. You cannot ask another person to do something you lack the courage to do yourself. Because a king is not a coward. They must make difficult decisions and do the things other people cannot.'*

He'd known his mother was right, that Dusk was in pain, and that this was a mercy. The dog was his, and asking someone else to grant that mercy because he was too afraid to do it himself was a coward's way out. And he wasn't a coward.

So he'd put his dog down. He'd forced himself to watch the life drain out of the animal's eyes and he'd felt as if he'd killed part of himself. But he'd learned a lesson that day and it wasn't just about making hard decisions and taking responsibility. It was also about how much love hurt.

Love had also been part of the decision he'd made later, to fight for the crown, and to take Yusuf's life, because he loved his country.

'You did the right thing', his mother had said after the fight, when Yusuf's body had been taken away. *'If you had not killed him, he would have killed you. And even if you had beaten him and let him live, he would have drawn sympathy. His supporters would have torn this country apart.'* Her expression had been like iron, the kind of iron she'd shaped in him. *'You were a surgeon, Khalil. He was a cancer that had to be cut out so our country could live. Do not spare him a single moment's thought.'*

But he'd spared him more than a single moment's thought. Because even though intellectually he'd known Yusuf had been planning to take the crown whether he won the battle for succession or not, and had been fomenting an insurrection that would have torn Al Da'ira apart, he'd never been able to quite suppress the doubt that had consumed him afterwards.

The battle was not supposed to end in death. It was supposed to end when one participant yielded, thereby accepting defeat. So when Yusuf had pulled out the knife he'd had hidden in the middle of their fight, making it clear that yielding was not an option, and that he meant to kill him, Khalil had not been expecting it. And it was only in that moment that the full horror of it had descended upon him: only one of them was going to make it out of the battle alive. And it could not be Yusuf. His country could not afford for it to be Yusuf. Which meant it had to be him.

He'd not felt like a surgeon then, or even the heir to the throne.

He'd felt like a killer.

The memories made something shudder and shift inside him, so he shoved them away. That was in the past and he couldn't change what had happened.

The most important thing was Sidonie and her happiness, and she needed to be happy for the sake of his people and for his country. He couldn't give her love, but perhaps he could give her that happiness. It was his responsibility after all.

Determination settled inside him.

He turned from the fountain and strode back inside to his bedroom. There, he went over to the huge, canopied bed where Sidonie was curled, fast asleep, and he got in, gathering her warm, sweet, naked body close.

She gave a little sigh and snuggled into him, her red hair spilling over his chest.

He tightened his arms around her.

Yes, he would make her happy. He would. If it was the very last thing that he did.

CHAPTER NINE

SIDONIE STOOD IN the deserted throne room of Khalil's palace, a thousand butterflies fluttering in her stomach.

When she'd woken this morning, Khalil hadn't been there, but Aisha had. The woman had delivered a raft of instructions on the day's schedule, and then she'd had breakfast brought to the King's apartments so that Sidonie could eat.

Sidonie hadn't felt much like eating—she'd been far too nervous—but she'd forced something down. Then Aisha had escorted her back to the Queens' apartments, where she was pounced upon by a fleet of servants who dressed her in a simple, unadorned gown of white silk that flowed like water over her curves and then out behind her in a long train.

She'd had no idea how he'd managed to find a gown that fitted her so perfectly on such short notice, but he had. And it was beautiful. Then they laid a veil over her face and hair, of white silk lace embroidered with tiny, glittering diamonds, and she loved that too.

Khalil clearly wasn't wasting any time, because then she was escorted through the echoing palace corridors that seemed to get grander and grander, until she was shown into a huge, ornately tiled room, its roof supported by many elegant columns.

The sun shone down through a hole in the roof in the very centre of the room, making the tiles glitter and bathing everything in light.

Sidonie was guided to that shaft of light and now she stood there, feeling as if she was standing in a waterfall of sunlight, waiting to be married. To Khalil.

Are you sure this is what you really want? He's not your Khalil, you know that.

No, but she wasn't his Sidonie either. They weren't the people they'd once been—five years apart and heartbreak had seen to that.

But what did that matter? She loved him, that was the constant, and as his wife she'd have the time to rebuild the relationship they'd once had. And anyway, she was stronger now than she'd been back then, and more certain. More than a match for the King he was.

What about love, though? What kind of marriage would you have without that?

But they did have love. Her love.

Will that ever be enough?

The thought brought memories, dim now after so long, but still there. Of her parents, her mother's warm hugs and her father tossing her in the air and making her laugh. They'd loved her. They'd loved her so much. And she'd ached for them after they'd died, ached for those moments of affection and tenderness, and she'd spent years hoping for the same from her aunt. But her aunt hadn't loved her and there had been no tenderness or affection from her, none at all.

Khalil might not love her, but he wanted her, and he cared about her, and he gave her pleasure. His touches set her on fire. He could give her affection and tenderness, too; it wasn't that he didn't.

It was enough.

Are you sure about that?

But the thought slid away as a tall figure strode through the gloom of the throne room, then stepped into the shaft of sunlight with her, bathing him in glory. And for a second she could understand why his court laid themselves on the floor and pressed their faces to the ground whenever he passed. Because in this moment he truly seemed divine.

There was a lump in her throat as she looked at him, and she had to blink back her tears.

He wore white, as she did—white shirt, loose white trousers and a white robe over his broad shoulders, heavily embroidered with gold thread. It glittered in the sunlight, a spectacular contrast to the smooth bronze of his skin and the inky blackness of his hair and eyes. And those eyes were fixed on her, a burning flame glowing in the darkness.

He didn't speak, merely raised his hand to her, and she walked towards him, drawn helplessly, reaching for his hand. His fingers wound through hers, warm and strong, and the nervous fluttering inside her settled.

This was right. This was what she'd wanted. What she'd always wanted. He didn't question it, so why should she? And, while she had no idea what this marriage would bring, she'd be strong enough to deal with it.

Are you sure? After all those years of letting your aunt walk all over you, hoping for a scrap of affection that she was never going to give? After he walked away from you and broke your heart?

Well, once they were married, he couldn't walk away, could he? She wouldn't let him.

Sidonie held tight to Khalil's hand as a priest appeared in the sunlight too, and then there was no more time for thinking as the ceremony began.

It was short and sweet and she said her vows in a steady voice, mirroring Khalil's deep tones of certainty as he said his. Then he pushed a narrow band of white gold studded with diamonds onto her finger and she did the same for him—his ring was simpler, with a single diamond in the centre.

Then the priest pronounced them husband and wife, and Khalil stepped towards her and with careful hands lifted her veil. There was a triumph in his eyes that stole her breath. Then he bent and kissed her, a hard, intense kiss. A claiming.

She was trembling as he lifted his head and turned to the priest, nodding and murmuring a word of thanks. The priest glided away, leaving her finally alone with her new husband in an echoing throne room.

It was done. Finally, he was hers and she was his.

Her gaze met his and she could see the satisfaction in it. He felt this rightness too, didn't he?

But you're just his trophy. His prize. His queen. You're not really his wife.

In those years where they'd been friends, she'd indulged herself in fantasies about marrying him. About their wedding day and his ring on her finger, and what their wedding night would be like. And in every one of those fantasies it had been love she'd seen in his eyes, not triumph. He'd told her he loved her, too. Saying the words in his deep, dark voice.

An icy thread of doubt curled through her, that perhaps loving him wasn't enough after all, that she needed more than that, but she shoved it away.

It was too late for doubts. They were married.

'I hope you did not mind the lack of ceremony,' Khalil said, reaching for her hand once again and closing his fingers around it. 'I did not want any witnesses other than the priest. This was just for you and me.'

'No,' she murmured, her voice not quite steady. 'I didn't mind at all. But…why the throne room?'

'It is customary. All royalty in Al Da'ira are married in the throne room.' He frowned at her. 'Your fingers are cold. Are you okay?'

The satisfaction in his expression had been replaced by concern, and it made her heart ache. He *did* care about her. He did. She wasn't just a prize he'd won.

'Just nerves,' she said, forcing a smile.

His gaze narrowed slightly as if he didn't believe her. But he didn't say anything else, merely tightening his grip as he walked towards the doors, drawing her along with him. 'No need to be nervous, *ya hayati*. I have something special planned.'

His hand was warm, so she concentrated on that, and not on the uncertainty that had gathered in her stomach. 'What something special?'

He glanced at her, his eyes dark as obsidian, and he flashed her a brief smile, a smile she remembered from years ago, so rare and yet so full of warmth that her heart turned over in her chest, banishing the doubt. 'You'll see.'

Yes, she could do this. Loving him would be enough. She didn't need him to love her in return. And who knew? Maybe one day he would, and everything would be fine.

She followed him as he strode into the ornate hallway just outside the throne room, palace guards falling into step with them.

They went up a great, sweeping staircase and then down a few more corridors, before coming out onto a large terrace that, given the helicopter sitting in the middle of it, must have been a helipad.

Guards were everywhere, flanking her and Khalil as he went straight to the machine and opened the door for her. 'Another helicopter ride, Khal?' She gave him a look from underneath her lashes. 'Let's hope there is actually dinner at the end of this one.'

Much to her surprise he laughed, the sound deep and warm and incredibly sexy. 'Oh, there will be many things at the end of this one, *ya hayati*. Dinner being the least of them.'

Five minutes later they were in the air, leaving behind the royal palace and Al Da'ira's capital city, and in another ten they were soaring above a starkly beautiful mountain range. Then, almost before Sidonie was ready, they were descending towards what looked like a small palace that stood on a mountain plateau, surrounded by a series of terraces and balconies.

Her heart kicked inside her chest. She'd never been here before, but she was certain she knew this place. It looked familiar to her in some way.

They landed on a helipad beside the little palace. It was cooler up in the mountains, a fresh but pleasant breeze lifting her veil as Khalil helped her out of the helicopter.

Royal servants were kneeling on the ground, their faces pressed to the stone as Khalil led Sidonie to the palace's doors.

'Khal,' she murmured, deciding that, since she was going to be Queen, she may as well start straight away. 'We could make a small change right now, couldn't we? They don't need to prostrate themselves.'

'They do not have to,' he murmured back. 'I told you that. Their beliefs require it.'

So he'd told her, yet she still didn't like it. 'But you're not a god. And if all of this is to build confidence in the throne after Amir, you have been ruling for five years. Surely they know you're not your father by now.'

He stared at her a moment, his expression unreadable. Then he glanced at the servants. 'You do not have to give me formal obeisance,' he said. 'That will not be required in future.'

Slowly the servants stirred then got to their feet, looking at Khalil cautiously.

'But, Majesty,' one old man said, 'you must have acknowledgement.'

Khalil frowned. 'Do you think that I am Amir? That I need this level of acknowledgment? That I demand it?' There was no heat in his voice. It was a simple question.

The man eyed him. 'No, Majesty. You are not him in any way. But we wish to honour you.'

There was another silence. Khalil's expression was oddly still. 'You can continue to serve me willingly,' he said at last. 'That is all the honour I need.'

A flicker of something that looked like respect passed across the old man's face. Then he bowed deeply. 'Your will, Majesty.'

Khalil inclined his head in acknowledgement but didn't say anything else. He reached for her hand, though, as they approached the palace doors, and he squeezed it gently. He'd liked what she'd said. He'd liked it a lot.

There was still hope for him.

The palace was made of white stone that gleamed against the black rock of the mountains, set off by the small, yet beautiful gardens that surrounded it. There were also colonnades and courtyards and airy arcades, the silence broken only by the sound of fountains playing.

It was absolutely beautiful.

'What is this place?' she asked as Khalil led her inside. 'It's gorgeous.'

'It was my mother's palace,' he said. 'I grew up here.'

So that was why it was familiar. He'd told her how his mother had been fiercely protective, yet very strict with him. And he'd had a harsh childhood.

Why would he want to come here?

She wanted to ask him, but then more servants approached and Khalil was murmuring instructions. Then he led her from the entrance hall and straight out through an atrium courtyard shaded with orange trees, with a small fountain and arched colonnade. He pulled open another door into a shady interior hall and up some stairs. Then he stopped before a simple wooden door and pushed it open, stepping into a large room. The walls were simply tiled in white and light blue, the floor of pale wood. High, arched windows gave a magnificent view of the mountains.

Though it wasn't the mountains that Sidonie noticed, not when the huge, canopied bed piled high with white cushions took up most of the room.

Khalil shut the door behind them, then shrugged off his white robe, leaving it to lie carelessly over a nearby chair. Then he looked at her and there was fire in his black eyes, and it blazed.

'Come here, wife,' he murmured, his voice getting darker and deeper.

Excitement gripped her, goosebumps rising on her skin, her heartbeat getting faster. So that was what he was impatient for. She should have known.

Not that she wasn't impatient too, even after the night before, when he'd kissed, tasted, and explored every inch of her body, before showing her how to do the same for him.

She wanted him. She wanted to finally claim him as her husband every bit as much as he wanted to claim her.

Slowly she walked over to where he stood, so tall and broad and beautiful in his white wedding clothing, then stopped in front of him. 'What can I do for you, my husband?'

A smile curved his beautiful mouth, a wicked smile that looked far too good on him. 'We have another custom in Al Da'ira. When a couple marry, on their wedding night the new wife undresses her husband so she may worship him.'

She had to smile. 'Sounds like a custom you've only just made up right now.'

He laughed, the sound so sexy she almost shivered. 'You are far too clear-sighted, Sidonie al Nazari. You see right through me.'

She stepped forward and lifted her hands to the buttons on his shirt, beginning to undo them, the sound of her new name settling something inside her.

'If I saw right through you, Your Majesty, I would know why you brought me here.' She glanced up at him. 'This place doesn't have happy memories for you, I know it doesn't. So why did you choose it for our honeymoon?'

Khalil was already so hard all he could think about was having his new wife's hands on him as quickly as possible. Everything had taken far longer than he'd either hoped or wanted, even though logically it had all happened as fast as it could.

Also, he'd wanted some degree of ceremony, because he knew Sidonie would like it. Hence the throne-room wedding in the shaft of sunlight, and the priest. Then coming here for their honeymoon…

He hadn't expected her to ask about it, though in retrospect he should have. He'd talked to her many times about his childhood here, though not about Dusk.

He tensed slightly despite himself. 'I wanted somewhere out of the way, where I could spend days with you without anyone else around.'

Lies. You shouldn't have brought her here if you didn't want to revisit the past.

Except he wasn't going to revisit the past, or at least he wasn't going to right now, not when he had other, more pleasant things he wanted to do.

Sidonie was looking up at him, puzzled almost. Her fingers were in the process of undoing a button on his shirt with maddening slowness, fingertips brushing his bare chest and winding his impatience even tighter, making him want to tear her hands away and take her right there on the floor.

But he didn't want their wedding night to start with such a loss of control. That would hardly set a good precedent. He wanted something slower and more sensual to mark the occasion.

It was difficult, though, to hang on to his patience when she was standing so close and he could smell her delicious scent, feel the seductive warmth of her body. She was so lovely in her white wedding gown, with her red hair loose and covered by the white veil, the diamonds sewn into it glittering like a scattering of raindrops.

How he'd always imagined her as his bride. His to claim. And even though he'd already done so, every instinct he had was urging him to do it again.

'I hope you do not want me to answer that now,' he said. 'Not when we have more important things to do.'

'Why not now?' She looked down at what she was doing, slowly undoing another button. 'You obviously brought us here for a reason.'

He gritted his teeth, his muscles tensing as she brushed his chest yet again, igniting fire along all his nerve-endings. 'Let me rephrase,' he said tightly. '*I* do not want to answer that question right now.'

'We have all night, Khal.' She undid the button and looked up at him again, her gaze searching. 'Or is there something you don't want to tell me?'

Telling her shouldn't matter. The things he'd done he'd done for the good of his nation. But this was their wedding night. It was hardly the time or the place for such confessions.

She should know. She should know what kind of man she married.

Tension coiled through him, though he didn't know why. She'd married a king, that was what he was, that was what he'd become. And he wasn't ashamed of what he'd had to do to be that king.

She must have sensed his tension because she frowned. 'There is something, isn't there? What is it?'

You doubt. Even now.

Once, he had. But he certainly didn't now. His doubt was a flaw he'd cut out of himself the night he'd walked away from Sidonie, along with the pain of leaving her, and the longing. Because Al Da'ira needed a strong king, a king without flaws, and so that was what he'd become.

Yusuf had been a sickness he'd had to cut out, a mercy he'd had to give, the same mercy he'd given Dusk.

Perhaps he should tell her after all. That way she would know exactly where she stood.

Her hands dropped. 'I don't have to—'

'Did I ask you to stop?' This wasn't going to be a pleasant conversation, but he wasn't going to let it ruin his wedding night. 'Keep doing what you were doing.'

She searched his face for a moment and then nodded, lifting her hands to push his shirt from his shoulders.

Cool air moved over his skin, but for some reason it didn't soothe him. Every part of him was tense. She stepped in closer and it was all he could do not to put his hands on her hips and pull against him. But touching her while he told her about all the… unpleasantness seemed wrong, so he kept them still.

'You know about the battle of succession. About the fight between the oldest children of my father's four wives.'

Sidonie's stroking fingers paused. 'Yes, I remember you telling me.'

'My grandfather changed it so that the fight was more ritualistic and no longer to the death.' He held her gaze. 'Again, I did not tell you to stop.'

She flushed then lifted her hands again, running the tips of her fingers along his collarbones. 'Yes, you told me about the fight, too. How your half-brother was injured.'

'He was not injured,' Khalil said flatly. 'Just before the fight, my mother had intelligence that Yusuf intended to kill me. He wanted the crown, and he was going to take it. He'd been planning insurrection and already had an army of followers waiting for his call.'

Sidonie's face paled, her eyes widening, and that tension inside him made him feel as if he was made of iron. He didn't understand why. His decision had been correct, the only one he could have made.

'He had brought a knife with him, so my mother secretly passed a knife to me so I would not be un-armed.' He remembered the weight of that knife too. 'It was important that I win the battle. Yusuf was…

too much like my father. He took pleasure in cruelty, and he wanted power. It would have been a disaster if he'd won the succession.'

Sidonie had gone white. 'Khalil…'

'Yusuf was not as good a fighter as I was,' he went on, making the words hard and cold, just as he himself was. 'Though he tried very hard to kill me.'

Her gaze darkened. 'But he didn't kill you. And obviously you won, since you're King.'

'I did win. But there was a cost.' The word 'cost' sounded ugly to him, as if a life had a monetary value. 'Only one of us was going to come out of that fight alive and I made the decision that it would be me.'

Sidonie stared up at him for a long moment, her gaze searching, and for once in his life he couldn't tell what she was thinking.

His heart was beating far too fast, all his muscles tense. He wished she hadn't had to hear this. He wished he hadn't had to tell her the truth. Everything about it had been dark and ugly, and he hadn't wanted her to know, because he hadn't wanted her to see him differently back then. He'd loved the way she saw him as just an ordinary person. But ordinary people didn't kill other people for their country's sake, not if they weren't soldiers.

'I killed him, Sidonie,' he went on, so there could be no doubt. 'I did it for my country. I had to. But that does not make what I did any less terrible.'

She contemplated him for a moment, then slowly she leaned into him and pressed a kiss to his throat, her lips warm and soft. 'I'm so sorry,' she breathed. 'I'm so sorry you had to make that decision.'

Her kiss should have relaxed him, should have made him burn with desire, and yet every muscle was rigid. Sorry. She was sorry. He didn't know what to do with that.

'You do not need to be sorry.' His voice was somehow rougher than it should have been and his grip on her hands had tightened. 'It was the correct decision.'

'This was before you came to Oxford, wasn't it?'

'Yes. I was eighteen.'

Sidonie's face was full of a terrible sympathy. 'You were so full of shadows back then. I used to wonder what haunted you, but you never talked about it, and I didn't want to push.'

'It did haunt me,' he said. 'But it does not now.'

Yet her gaze was very steady, looking at him as if she could see things he couldn't. 'Yes,' she said slowly. 'Yes, I think it still does.'

Shock went through him like a lightning strike, shaking something inside him. 'Why would you say that?'

'Because I can see it in your eyes.' Her green gaze held his, that sympathy still shining there. 'You didn't want to tell me, did you? You wanted me to keep on believing that Yusuf had only been injured.'

'I did not want to tell you because—'

'You brought me here, Khal. You wanted me to know your past. And you wanted me to know, because no matter how you deny it, it does haunt you.'

Another shock hit him, harder this time. 'That is not true.'

'Isn't it?' Sidonie pulled one hand from his grip and touched his face gently. 'You don't have to pretend. I've known you for ten years and besides, I'm your wife. You can be strong for your people, but you don't have to be strong with me.'

For some reason her touch hurt, shaking that thing inside him, the lump of rock that he'd turned his heart into. That rock he'd *had* to turn his heart into because he couldn't allow it to be anything other than stone.

He gripped her wrist, wanting to pull her fingers from his cheek and yet for some reason not being able to. 'A king cannot afford doubts,' he said harshly. 'A king cannot be haunted by anything.'

Yet you still have those doubts. You didn't want to take his life, just as you didn't want to take the life of your dog.

She didn't speak, just looked at him, her gaze full of a tenderness that stopped his breath.

'Kings have to make difficult decisions,' he heard himself say, the urge to explain himself too strong to ignore. 'They have to do terrible things in order to protect people. They need to be strong and certain, and they cannot second-guess themselves. I made the decision I had to make and I took action. So no, it does not haunt me.'

There was a strange sheen in Sidonie's eyes. 'Then why are you so tense? You're holding my wrist so tightly.'

Another icy wave washed over him. He forced his fingers to open, to let her go, even though every part of him felt as if he was desperate for the touch of her skin.

You are hurting her. You are always hurting her.

He took a step back from her, putting some distance between them, forcing away the strange desperation and trying to master himself. His heart was too loud in his head, and he couldn't bear the look in her eyes.

You should not have married her. She undermines everything you were taught.

No, that wasn't true. Marrying her had been the right decision. It was all those old feelings she brought back that was the issue. The feelings he thought he'd cut away years ago and somehow hadn't.

It wasn't her fault. It was his. It was his father's poisonous blood in his veins, the greed and selfishness threatening to overtake him. He had to be stronger than it, he had to be.

The pressure was back in his chest, as if that lump of stone was getting heavier and heavier, an aching weight that felt as if it would crush the air from his lungs.

It was doubt, that weight. Doubt that he had made the right decision in marrying her. Doubt that he'd done the right thing in even bringing her here.

You will never make her happy. Never.

She hadn't wanted to be here, yet he'd forced her. He'd essentially kidnapped her then seduced her into staying and marrying him. And he'd told himself over and over again that it was for his country, just as he'd told himself over and over again that Yusuf's death had been for his country, too. That he'd had to die. Just as Dusk had to die.

But that wasn't true, was it? Those were lies he'd told himself. Because if he'd truly thought that Yusuf had had to die, he wouldn't still have these doubts. The same doubts that had consumed him after Dusk's death, that perhaps it hadn't been a mercy after all. Perhaps it had been his own suffering he'd wanted to ease, not his dog's.

Perhaps all of it had been for himself.

You are just the same as Amir.

Sidonie's lovely face was full of concern, though she didn't come any closer. 'What is it, Khal?' she asked softly. 'You look upset. Please, let me help you.'

'I am not upset,' he forced out, his voice sounding as if it was coming from far away. 'But I understand if you cannot now go through with this wedding night.'

'Why would I not want to go through with it?'

'You don't care that I killed a man?' He didn't understand why she was looking at him as if it didn't matter and he didn't understand why it even mattered to him. 'You don't see me any differently?'

'No. You didn't do it for no reason, Khal. You were defending yourself. And you did what you thought was the right thing for your country and your people.' Slowly she walked towards him, closing the distance between them. 'And you didn't want to do it, did you?'

He felt rooted to the spot, unable to move as she came closer, and then she was there, raising her hands and placing her palms on his bare chest, her skin warm against his. Making the stone around his heart crack, letting all that poisonous doubt seep out. 'No,' he heard himself say hoarsely. 'I did not. But there should be no reason to doubt. It was the right thing to do. The only decision to make.'

'You were very young, Khal. And you took a life you didn't want to take. Anyone would be affected by that. Anyone would be haunted.'

He looked down into her eyes. 'That was not the only life I took.'

Shock flickered in her eyes. 'What?'

Another decision he'd had to make. Another decision he couldn't doubt and yet…there seemed to be nothing but doubt in him now.

'My mother's job was to bring me up strong in order to be a good king. But she was always afraid that my father's blood ran too hot in me. She believed that strength lay in being hard, and cold, and certain. That emotion clouded thinking, made a man weak. I had a dog and he got very sick, and there was nothing that could be done to save him. So, my mother decided he would be a good lesson for me. She gave me a knife and told me that if I wanted to be a strong king, to be responsible for others, I had to learn how to make difficult decisions. And that I could not ask another to do what I was too afraid to do myself.'

A horrified expression had crossed Sidonie's face, the sheen back in her eyes. Tears. They were tears. 'Oh, Khal… Did she make you put him down yourself?'

She knows the truth of you now. You did not have to make that decision and yet you did. You have horrified her.

The weight in his heart, the doubt, became even heavier, crushing the life out of him.

'Yes,' he said hoarsely, unable to stop himself. 'Dusk was sick. It was a mercy.'

'But you don't believe that, do you?'

He couldn't keep it all inside. 'Mercy should not hurt, yet it was the most painful thing I have ever done. And I could not help thinking that I did it to ease my own suffering, not my dog's.'

A tear escaped, running down her cheek, and he thought she would pull away from him, and he didn't know what he would have done if she had. But she didn't. Instead she lifted her hands to take his face between her palms, and it shocked him so much that she should want to touch him after what he'd told her that he couldn't move. 'Oh, Khal,' she said huskily. 'Of course it was painful. You loved your dog. He was sick and you were only a child. You shouldn't have been made to do that.'

He lifted his hands to hers, wanting to pull them away and yet wanting at the same time to keep them exactly where they were. 'My mother's intentions were good. She wanted to make me strong because she believed I would make the best King. That I would save Al Da'ira from my father. But I was also my father's son, and she did not want me to turn into him.'

Sidonie didn't say anything then, merely rising on her toes and brushing her mouth against his, silencing him once again. 'You're not him,' she said against his lips. 'You're just not, Khal, and you never were. Your people think so too. Remember what that old man said to you just before? He didn't think you were Amir, so why torture yourself with this?'

He gripped her tightly, his heart beating faster, harder, the doubt inside him eating away at his foundations, weakening him. 'Because Amir was a flawed man. A greedy and selfish man. Everything he did was for himself. So how am I any different? What if I took Yusuf's life because I wanted the way clear to be King? What if I took Dusk's because I hated to see him suffer and did not want to deal with it any more?'

Her hands gripped his face, holding him tightly, her green gaze on his, suddenly fierce. 'You *are* different, Khal. You have *always* been different. You're protective and generous, and you care about people so much. You don't want what's best for you. You want what's best for your people. But your problem, my darling husband, is that you're too rigid. Your standards for yourself are so high. And I think you're trying to be this strong, semi-divine king because you're too afraid to be a man.'

'That is not true. I am—'

'It is true. Doubts are normal. Doubts make you

human. And you're a wonderful, special human. A good man, a kind man. Yusuf, your dog…they were things you did because you felt you had to, but those things don't change who you are inside.' She let him go and put her palms back on his chest, pressing down. 'Your heart is still the same. You're the kindest man I've ever known, the kindest person.' Yet more tears were escaping and were running down her cheek even as the warmth of her palms seeped into him, easing the jagged ache inside him. 'And you're a good king. You held your country together through all those years of unrest, and you want what's best for it. You want what's best for your people.'

'A good king would not doubt himself.'

'No.' Sidonie gave him a smile through her tears. 'Doubt makes the best kings, you idiot. Don't you know that? It shows he cares, and you have to care, Khal. That's why you're different from your father and you always will be. It's because you care about other people, not because you don't.'

He stared at her, smiling at him despite those tears on her cheeks, feeling a kind of slow-dawning shock. He didn't know about all the other things she'd said about him, but what she'd said about doubt…resonated. He'd been taught that certainty was strength, and so he'd pushed away his doubts, crushed them, cut them out so there was nothing left in him but the strength he needed to rule.

He'd never thought that perhaps a king might need that doubt. He'd never thought that a king should care. His mother had told him that it was a weakness, not a strength, and yet… Perhaps Sidonie was right. His mother's intentions had been good, but she'd been rigid in her way. Her father hadn't treated her well and she had come to hate him in the end.

After all, his father really hadn't cared about his people or his country, and look what had happened to Al Da'ira.

He wanted to be a better king than that, he always had, but what if that meant admitting that he was just as full of doubt as the next person?

This is how she will change things. By changing you.

That fractured stone around his heart shifted again, making him ache for something he couldn't name. An ache that puzzled him when what he truly wanted was already standing right in front of him.

All he knew was that the tension that had gripped him wasn't there any more, and now all he could think about was her. He wanted his new wife and he wanted her now.

He took one of her hands in his and lifted it to his mouth, gently biting the tip of it and making her eyes go very wide. 'You are always wise, *ya hayati*. And I will have to think about what you have said. But… it is our wedding night, and, since you have not left me as I thought you would, I would like very much for you to continue the job you started.'

CHAPTER TEN

THE GENTLE NIP on her finger had sent a shockwave of sensation through her, and she was very conscious, all of a sudden, that he was shirtless, the wide, muscled expanse of his bronzed chest right in front of her.

Her husband.

He was so much more complicated than she'd ever guessed. She'd thought he'd told her everything about himself and yet he'd been holding on to those secrets. Those terrible, painful secrets. Secrets that had hurt him so badly.

It made her heart ache.

'I know,' she said softly. 'But I wish you had told me those things years ago. You didn't need to torture yourself for so long with them.'

'I did not want to tell you. I thought you would see me differently if I did. And I…could not have borne that back then.'

She blinked back the tears that kept filling her eyes. 'I would never have seen you differently. Not even back then.' And she wouldn't have. Because she'd told him the truth. Granting mercy to his sick dog was an act of kindness, though naturally it would haunt him. And as for Yusuf… No wonder he'd been tortured by that too.

He wasn't a killer. He'd just been forced into a situation that required him to defend himself, and that had had consequences.

It would be terrible if he *hadn't* doubted.

Khalil shook his head. 'You were everything bright, everything beautiful back then, Sidonie. You were the only happiness I'd ever known. I did not want to risk losing that for anything.'

Her throat ached and she wanted to tell him right then and there that he wouldn't have lost it, because she'd loved him then and she loved him still.

But this was already painful enough without bringing love into it.

What she wanted was to give him comfort, help him in any way she could, and she knew the best way to do that. He'd been waiting long enough.

'And you won't lose it now either,' she said quietly, dropping her hands to the buttons on his trousers, and she held his gaze as she undid those one by one, watching the flames start to ignite his sharp black eyes.

'You want me to worship you, husband?' She pulled open his fly. 'Then let me worship you.'

She went to her knees in front of him, dealt with his shoes first, then eased his trousers down, along with his underwear. He stepped out of the fabric and kicked it aside, standing before her completely naked, a sculpture of the perfect man cast in bronze.

Sidonie's mouth dried. He had shown her what to do for him the previous night, but this was their wedding night and she wanted to worship him as he should be worshipped, show him how much he meant to her, that nothing of what he'd told her changed the way she felt about him.

She put her hands on his powerful thighs, but then he reached down, taking her chin in a firm grip and tilting her head back so she could look at him.

His gaze was dark and very serious. 'You still want this? Even after what I told you?'

She could see the doubt in his eyes, but while he might doubt himself, she didn't. She knew who he was deep down. She'd spent ten years knowing him. And she knew his worth.

'Nothing's changed, Khal,' she said, putting the strength of her conviction into each word. 'For ten years you made me feel as if I wasn't just a lonely, unwanted orphan. You made me feel as if I was more, as if I was special.' The flame in his eyes glittered and his grip on her chin tightened. He looked as if he was going to say something more, but she pulled away gently. 'So now you need to be quiet and let me make you feel special too.' Then she pressed her lips to his stomach and began to work her way down.

The breath hissed out of him and when she reached to take the long, thick length of his sex in her hand, he muttered a low curse. And when she put her mouth on him and tasted him, worshipped him, he slid his fingers into her hair, the veil sliding off it and onto the floor, and held her tight.

He was a man full of doubt, but she wanted him to know that it didn't matter to her. That he was her husband and when she'd agreed to be his wife, when she'd married him, it was because he was that man. That friend. Not some kind of semi-divine king.

So she put the strength of her conviction into the way she stroked and tasted and explored him, until finally he groaned and pulled her to her feet. 'I need to be inside you,' he growled. 'Now.' Then he tore the gown from her body, along with her underwear, and picked her up and put her on the bed. And he followed her down, spreading her thighs with his strong hands and without hesitation thrusting deep inside her.

She gasped as pleasure bloomed like a flower, and she closed her legs around his waist, reaching for him to bring him close. His mouth came down on hers and then they were moving together, fast and desperate, clinging to each other as the storm broke around them and washed them away.

In the aftermath, lying beneath his hot, hard body, her arms around him, trembling like a leaf and feeling the aftershocks shake him too, Sidonie knew deep in her heart that she'd made the right decision in marrying him.

The thought of leaving him was unfathomable. It had broken her the first time he'd walked away from her and she wasn't going to let it happen again.

She loved him with a fierce, true love. And those doubts she'd had before?

She didn't feel them now. So what if she was his prize, his trophy? So what if he never talked about love or gave it to her?

Her love was enough for both of them, she knew it down to her bones.

Finally, Khalil moved, pressing his mouth to her throat and beginning to kiss his way down her body. It was clear he didn't want to talk any more and that was okay with her. She didn't want to talk either. Her realisation could wait, and besides, there had been enough revelations for one day. They could afford some time to relax and simply enjoy each other.

So she lay back and let her new husband do what he wanted with her.

As it turned out, it was exactly what she wanted too.

Khalil came to the wide French doors that opened out onto a shady terrace, stopped, then leaned on the doorframe.

Sidonie was lying on a low outdoor sofa piled high with pillows, dressed only in a loose robe of green silk. She had a book beside her, but it was clear she wasn't reading it because she looked to be fast asleep.

No wonder. He'd been keeping her up very late at night and waking her early in the morning. A hunger had set in inside him and he couldn't get enough of her. It was bordering on obsession and normally he wouldn't have permitted it, but, since she was his wife and this was their honeymoon, he allowed it.

Eventually it would wear off, he assumed, then they could settle into their marriage.

It had been three days since their wedding and he knew that soon he was going to have to get back to the palace and resume the task of ruling his country, but he wanted a few more days alone with his wife.

He shifted against the doorframe, watching a breeze lift the edge of Sidonie's robe, exposing a pale expanse of thigh, and his body responded with predictable speed. But he didn't move, content to stand there for a few minutes longer, watching her.

He couldn't stop thinking about what she'd said to him on their wedding night, about how he was a good king and that doubt would only make him better. He still wasn't sure about that—his mother's teachings would take a while to unlearn—but what he was sure about was that she was wise, his Sidonie. So very perceptive.

She knew now the worst parts of him, and she hadn't turned away. She'd only looked up at him with those beautiful green eyes of hers and told him that those things didn't change the person he was inside. That he was a good man.

She also called you rigid and afraid to be a man.

That was true, and maybe she was right. But he had to be rigid. And it wasn't fear, it was necessity. He couldn't be the King he needed to be otherwise.

But maybe he could be a man with her. He could try at least.

Sidonie stirred on the couch, and he pushed himself away from the doorframe, moving over to where she lay, that heavy, aching feeling in his chest getting stronger. It was there all the time now and he still didn't know what it was. But only being near her eased it. Yes, he needed her, and he probably always would.

Carefully, he sat on the couch beside her and brushed a strand of red hair off her cheek, tucking it behind her ear. She smiled and her eyes opened. 'Hmm. I was having the loveliest dream and now I'm awake I realise it wasn't a dream at all. Because here you are.'

The heavy ache in his chest was getting painful now.

He ignored it, smiling back at her. 'Keep dreaming, *ya hayati*. I will make it even more pleasant for you.'

She gave a soft laugh and turned over onto her back, the silk robe shifting and clinging in the most delectable places. He was growing even harder, especially when she gave a sexy, sensual little stretch, her back arching. 'Again, Khal?'

He reached down and traced the curve of one full breast with light fingertips. 'Do you object?'

'Of course not.' The look she gave him from underneath her lashes was smouldering. 'I might even have to insist.'

It was his turn to laugh then, because she was beautiful and he loved it when she flirted with him, and the expression on her face softened. The glow in her eyes became somehow more intense and the smile that curved her mouth took on a warmth that nearly stopped his heart.

'I love you, Khalil ibn Amir al Nazari,' she said quietly. 'I love you so much.'

She had said those words to him once before, years ago on a snowy street in Soho. And the effect they'd had then was the same as it was now, the words cutting through him like a sword through silk, opening him up.

And they should not have done. He had hardened himself thoroughly since that night. He was different. He'd changed. He shouldn't have felt as if all his insides were spilling out, pain gripping him.

Your fault. You should have talked to her about this. You should have told her that marrying her had nothing to do with love, and that love was something you couldn't allow.

He felt cold. They should have had that discussion. But she'd distracted him with sex the night before, and then he'd been so impatient to marry her he hadn't had time for yet more talking. And last night, there had been all those painful confessions and afterwards, when she'd touched him, all he'd wanted was the warmth of her body and the comfort only she could give.

You have been selfish. Greedy. Like Amir.

Yes, he had been.

'I have been meaning to have that discussion with you,' he said flatly, the knowledge sitting in his gut like a stone. 'Love is not part of this marriage, Sidonie. It will never be part of it.'

The look on her face didn't change despite his tone, her gaze very steady. Not at all the same as five years earlier, when there had been only fearful hope in her eyes. 'Why not?' she asked.

The cold inside him deepened, though he tried to force it away. 'Because I do not want it.'

'I see. Because why? Love is not permitted for kings?'

It was impossible to read the expression on her face.

'It is not.' He tried to keep his voice even.

'I didn't say you had to love me,' she said. 'I only said that I love you.'

'No.' He hadn't even realised he'd pushed himself off the couch until he found himself standing a few paces away, staring at her, as if he wanted to put some distance between them. 'We should have talked about this, and I am sorry that I did not. But no, there can be no love between us.'

Sidonie was sitting up now, the green robe gathered around her, red hair falling in a pretty waterfall over her shoulders. She was still looking at him with the same terrible certainty. 'Why? What is so very threatening about the fact that I love you? Tell me what's going through your head.'

'Why do you think?' His voice was hoarse. 'Because I do not love you back, Sidonie.'

She lifted a shoulder as if it wasn't a big deal.

'So? I didn't ask for you to love me. That's not why I said it.'

'Then why did you say it?' The words came out sharp, full of edges, like razor wire, and he was breathing very fast. 'Five years ago, you said it to me, and I broke your heart. That is what you told me... I walked away from you then because I could not give you what you wanted. And nothing has changed, Sidonie. I still cannot.'

He couldn't. There were already cracks in the stone around his heart, the doubt inside him deepening. He could not love her back because love was a weakness that undermined his strength. And he was supposed to make her happy, that was what he'd promised himself.

No. That's a lie you told yourself. This hasn't got anything to do with what kings are and aren't permitted. You want to love her, but love makes you do such terrible things.

He'd loved his country, so he'd killed Yusuf. He'd loved Dusk, so he'd killed him too. And all those years ago, he'd once loved Sidonie. And he'd walked away from her, dealing her a mortal blow.

There was a weight around his heart, crushing him, suffocating him.

'It doesn't matter,' Sidonie said. 'It doesn't matter that nothing's changed. I told you because even kings need someone who loves them.' Her red brows drew together. 'Why is that so bad?'

She didn't understand. Which meant he would have to tell her. 'Because I do not love you,' he repeated. 'And I *never* will, Sidonie. *Never.* I am too much like my father. I have his blood in me.'

He wouldn't do it again. He couldn't. The blood inside him was too strong and his hunger for Sidonie was too intense. He had to keep his emotional distance, he *had* to. He didn't know what would happen if he didn't.

Sidonie pushed herself off the couch and crossed the space between them, the green robe flowing around her, making her look the goddess of spring that he'd hoped to give his people. And the terrible, crushing ache in his chest squeezed tighter.

'You're not listening,' she said calmly, coming up to him and putting her hands on his chest, smoothing the black cotton of the robe he wore. 'It doesn't matter.'

He couldn't bear for her to touch him, it felt too painful. So he took her wrists in his hands and pulled her fingers away from him. 'It may not matter to you, but it matters to me.'

Still she didn't look upset. 'Why?'

He didn't want to spell it out to her, but it seemed as if he was going to have to. 'You lost your parents, Sidonie. You lost the two people who cared about you most in the world, and you were raised instead by that awful aunt of yours.' He looked down into her eyes. 'Tell me that you don't want to be loved. Tell me that you don't need it like you need air to breathe. Tell me and make me believe it.'

Finally, her gaze flickered. 'I don't. You're what's important to me.'

She was lying to herself, but that didn't matter. He already had his answer. 'But I should not be. What you want matters, *ya hayati*. You should not be putting what you need second all the time. You do not deserve it.'

She didn't try to pull her hands away and she didn't try to touch him again. 'It seems to me that I should be the one who gets to decide what I deserve, not you. Just like I get to decide what's important and what's not. Yes, I lost my parents. Yes, my aunt was awful. But then I met a wonderful man who became my friend, and he showed me what I deserved, and I decided that what I deserved was him.'

'I broke your heart,' he said desperately. 'That is what you said.'

'You did,' she said. 'But you won't do again. I know you won't.'

'How? How do you know that? You know nothing of the man I have become, nothing about the sacrifices I have made for my country. What is to say that one day I will not sacrifice you too?'

'Of course I know about your sacrifices,' she shot back. 'You told me about them, remember? And don't tell me I don't know you. I've known you for ten years and, while we've both changed, we're still who we were deep down inside. I told you last night what kind of man you are, the kind of man you've always been, so yes, I know you. And you'd never break my heart, not again.'

He tightened his grip, pulling her against him. 'But am I not doing it now? Telling you I can never love you while you pour all your love into me? You giving me everything while I give you nothing in return? How is that not breaking your heart into pieces?'

She went pale. 'But given time I can—'

'Did time work with your aunt?' It was a low blow but he had to make her see. 'Did that ever change her?'

Her lovely green eyes glittered. 'You are not my aunt.'

He dropped her wrists and stood there, rigidly, covering up the fractures in the stone around his heart, holding on to what he knew to be true, to the certainty, that *this* was the right decision to make. The only decision. And not for himself, but for her. 'No, I am not. And I will not be her. I will not hold you to me when I cannot give you what you need to be happy. And I want you to be happy, Sidonie. I want you to be free to choose for yourself, to have someone who will love you the way you deserve to be loved.'

Her chin lifted, her back straight and proud. 'But I have chosen. And I choose you.'

Every part of him was tense. 'Then you have chosen poorly.'

And before she could say anything else, he turned and stalked back to the house.

CHAPTER ELEVEN

SIDONIE WATCHED KHALIL stride away from her, feeling her heart fracture into a million tiny pieces.

It was happening again. She'd told him the truth and he'd walked away the way he had five years earlier.

Your own fault. You should never have told him you loved him.

It had been a risk, she'd known that. But when he'd smiled at her, looking like the man he'd been years before, she hadn't been able to stop herself.

He was her husband and she loved him, and she wanted him to know that. After the truths of the night before, she'd thought he deserved to know that nothing had changed her feelings for him, and that nothing ever would. She loved him unreservedly, accepting him for everything he was, the way he'd accepted her, and she couldn't bear for him to think that somehow he was unworthy of it, or didn't deserve it after the things he'd done.

She didn't know what she expected, but she hadn't thought history would repeat itself.

'So that's it?' She didn't raise her voice. She didn't need to. He would hear. 'I tell you that I love you and your answer is to walk away? This is so five years ago, Khalil.'

He stopped dead right before the French doors, his back to her, his black robe swirling around him.

'If you want my happiness so badly, explain to me how that is going to fill me with joy?' she went on, since he didn't look as if he was going to. 'You did this last time too, making me feel as if this was all my fault somehow.'

'No, that is not…' His deep voice sounded ragged, and she very much wanted to cross the distance and put her arms around him, but she wasn't going to. Not this time. 'That is not what I am saying.'

'So, if I had never told you everything would be fine?' Anger was filling her now, the anger she'd never let herself truly feel years ago, an anger that she'd fought down and pushed away, hidden under the milder layers of irritation and annoyance. The anger that her aunt had never allowed her. The anger she should have given him five years ago and hadn't. 'That our marriage would be full of bliss if only I hadn't mentioned the L word?'

He was silent, his back rigid, his wide shoulders tense. Then he turned around, and her breath caught. The expression on his beautiful face wasn't impenetrable or hard to read now, no, she could read every line. He looked as if he was in agony. 'Sidonie, that is not what I am—'

'*No*,' she shouted suddenly. 'No, *you're* the one

who's not listening to *me*.' Then, before she could stop herself, she stormed up to him, stopping inches away from him as he stared at her with tortured dark eyes. 'I can't believe you'd tell me all those lies about how you can't love me, and you want me to be happy, only to walk away from me *again*.' She stared fiercely back, letting him see her anger. 'You're a coward, Khalil. That's the real issue. It's not that you can't love me or that kings aren't permitted love. It's that you won't love me. Because you are afraid.'

'It is *not* fear.'

'Then what is it?' she demanded. 'What is so very bad about loving me, Khalil?'

He looked as if he was going to come apart at the slightest touch, anguish bleeding out of him. He took a step so they were almost touching. 'Because you broke me.' His voice was ragged and hoarse. 'Because you broke my heart, too. I loved you, but I could not have you. And I cannot… I *will* not…let myself be broken again.'

It was the truth; she could see it in his eyes. She could feel it in her own heart, the shattering pain that had torn them apart all those years ago.

Leaving her *had* broken him, and he was protecting himself now, just as she had.

If she'd been the woman she'd been five years earlier, she'd have softened. She'd have put her arms around him and told him that it was okay, he could protect himself. She didn't need to be loved back and being married to him was enough.

But it wasn't enough. She understood that now and he'd made her see it.

She couldn't spend the years of her marriage pouring her soul into a man who was too afraid to love her in return. Because she knew what would happen if she did. She'd lived it already with her aunt.

She'd become smaller, quieter. She'd push her own thoughts and feelings and wants and needs right down. She'd become weaker. A faded, washed-out version of the woman she was now.

The woman she'd become because of this man.

She didn't want to lose that woman. That woman was strong and passionate and brave. That woman had learned to ask for what she wanted, and if she was going to hold on to her she couldn't give in now.

Because deep down she knew, in her heart, that Khalil wanted her. That he needed her. And she thought that maybe he loved her too, but that was something he'd have to choose himself.

She'd stopped protecting herself and had stepped into her truth. Now it was his turn.

It was a risk to do this, to insist, but she had to do it.

For both their sakes.

'Then leave.' She took a step back. 'Go on, run away, Khalil. You're so very good at doing that, after all. If you're not brave enough to bear loving me and having me love you in return, then you're not the man I thought you were.'

He stood there, staring at her, his black eyes burning in his proud, sharp features.

But she wasn't going to wait for him to walk away from her, not this time.

So it was she who strode past him, and went into the house without a backward glance.

Khalil didn't want to stay while she was there. So he ordered a helicopter to be brought, and when it arrived he got on it.

He couldn't bear to be near her. Couldn't bear her fierce determination to love him. Or the way she'd flung that accusation straight in his face: *you're a coward.*

It wasn't fear that drove him away, couldn't she see that? He had to protect himself. Walking away from her the last time had broken him so utterly that he'd had to destroy the person he'd been just to survive.

And he had to survive. For his nation and his crown. If not then everything he'd ever done—Dusk, Yusuf—would have been for nothing.

He couldn't allow that to happen to him again. He couldn't.

The helicopter finally landed and he got out, dismissing his servants and striding for his apartments. He needed time to think about what to do next, because for the first time in his life he didn't know. He had no idea.

There, he tried to involve himself in work, but he couldn't concentrate. None of the decisions he had to make seemed right and he doubted every one. He doubted everything, including himself.

She'd told him doubt would make him a better king, but he didn't see how, not when he couldn't make any decisions. It seemed impossible.

He poured himself a neat vodka, a taste he'd developed over the past couple of years, and threw it down, relishing the burn. Hoping for some clarity, even though he knew drinking wasn't going to give him the kind of clarity he wanted.

Sure enough, after a couple of hours, he found himself sitting on the couch where he'd first taken Sidonie, the heavy, aching feeling sitting there like an elephant sitting on his chest. Making it hard to breathe, making it hard to even think.

His phone went off and he grabbed at it, staring down at the screen, wanting it to be Sidonie for some reason. But it wasn't. It was Galen.

He didn't want to answer it, but he did anyway. 'What?' he demanded gracelessly.

'Hmm,' Galen said. 'You sound like you're in a good mood.'

'Did you want something, Galen?'

'It's about your marriage celebration ball… I was thinking—'

'There will be no celebration,' Khalil cut him off tersely. 'I have decided it is a bad idea.'

There was a silence down the other end of the phone.

'Any particular reason?' Galen asked, his tone neutral.

And Khalil didn't know why he said what he said next. Perhaps it was because Galen had been through this and he knew what it was to have a woman love him. And he'd found it difficult, too. 'I do not know what to do,' Khalil said bleakly. 'She loves me, Galen. She told me so. But I cannot make her happy and she deserves it. She deserves it more than anyone I have ever met.'

There was another long silence. Then Galen said, 'You married her, didn't you?'

'Yes.'

'And do you love her?'

'I cannot.' He took a breath, the memory of what he'd flung at her in desperation resounding in his head. 'I…loved her before. But I could not have her and I…'

'You what?'

He could feel it inside him again, that pain. The same pain that had torn him when he'd had to put Dusk down. The same doubt and grief that had fractured him after Yusuf. 'It broke me,' he said starkly.

'Ah,' Galen said. 'I am familiar with that kind of break.'

Khalil shut his eyes, Sidonie in her green gown right there in front of him. Blazing with all that beautiful fury and passion. Telling him he was a coward and how dared he walk away from her a second time?

How could you? How could you break her heart again?

'She called me a coward,' he heard himself say. 'She called me a coward and walked away from me. And she was right. I barely survived losing her the first time. I do not think I could go through it again.'

'I know,' Galen said, no amusement in his tone now. 'It's hard. But ask yourself what you want, what you *really* want. And whether that's more important to you than anything else in your life.'

Khalil let out a breath. 'More important than my crown?'

'Yes,' Galen said without hesitation. 'A crown is just a thing. Someone else can wear it. And you don't cease to exist just because you're not a king. But will you cease to exist without her?'

Khalil stared at the wall, the words echoing inside him, resonating like a note with a tuning fork.

What did he want? What did he really, truly want? More than anything else in his life?

You know what you want. You've known it all along. And she was right. You went to England for her and you married her. You brought her back to your mother's house and you told her your secrets. And it's not for your country. It's not for your crown. It's not even for your own gratification. You brought her back because you lived without her for five years and you can't live like that any longer.

The truth of the thought hit him like lightning. Like a bullet from a gun. Shattering the stone around his heart, setting him free.

He loved her. He'd always loved her. He'd loved her for every second of those five years and that was why it had broken him, why he'd retreated so rigidly into the strictures of his kingship.

He'd loved her and he'd thought he couldn't have her, and the pain had torn him apart. The only way he'd been able to cope had been to tell himself he didn't feel it. To cut out his heart and get rid of it.

Galen was still talking. 'It's not easy, as I think I said to Augustine when I realised I was in love with Solace. Facing up to my fear was one of the hardest things I've ever done in my life, but I did. Because without Solace I was nothing and I knew it.' There was a pause and then he added quietly, 'It's worth it, Khal. Believe me, it's worth every second of pain.'

Yet he'd already had too much pain and so had his Sidonie.

She was more important to him than anything in his life. More important than his crown and more important than his country. Without them he would still exist.

But he couldn't exist without her. And if she was brave enough to love him, then he had to be brave enough to love her back.

'Galen,' he said roughly, 'I think I have just made a terrible mistake.'

'Thought you might say that,' Galen murmured. 'Then you'd better fix it, hadn't you?'

'Yes,' Khalil said and dropped the phone.

He didn't even waste time ending the call.

It was dark, but Sidonie sat still on the terrace, even as the wind became colder, the stars wheeling in the night sky above her head. She was thinking of plans and discarding them, trying to decide what to do about Khalil.

She didn't know whether he'd come back, and

she was on the point of deciding that she would just go to him, when she heard the sound of a helicopter overhead. Returning. And her heart squeezed tight in her chest.

Then five minutes later a man strode onto the terrace, still in the robes he'd worn when he'd left that morning, and he came over to where she sat. And before she could say anything, he knelt at her feet and looked up at her.

'My queen,' he said roughly. 'Will you forgive me?'

She was trembling all of a sudden. 'For what?'

'For leaving you. For walking away from you again.' His face was stripped bare of any of his usual guards and there was nothing but naked desire and a burning, fierce need that lit his eyes like stars. 'For being a coward. Because you were right. I was afraid. The way I left you in London hurt so much. It tore me apart. And that is what I have been afraid of ever since. I never wanted my heart to be so at risk again. But…another good friend of mine asked me what I wanted more than anything else. What was more important to me than even my crown.' He reached for her hand and held it gently in his, her wedding ring glittering in the starlight. 'And I realised that it is you, Sidonie al Nazari. Without my crown, I am just another man. But without you, I am nothing. I have only been half-alive these past five years, barely existing, and I am tired of it. I loved you back then, and I told myself many times that I could not possibly love you now. But I was wrong. I love you, *ya hayati.* My life. You were my sunshine back then and you still are. You always will be.'

She didn't mean to cry and yet a tear escaped, running down her cheek. 'I didn't want to walk away from you, Khal. I didn't. But I wanted you to choose for yourself.'

In the darkness he smiled, and took her other hand, turning both of them up. 'You are so very wise.' Then he kissed one palm and then the other. 'And so, I have chosen. It is you, my beautiful Sidonie. You are my life, my heart. You are my soul. And until death and beyond I am yours.'

There were more tears on her cheeks—she couldn't stop them, joy lighting up inside her. 'Now, that's a romantic proposal,' she said huskily, and then, since she couldn't stand it any more, she pulled her hands away and tugged him to his feet. 'Kiss me, you idiot.'

He laughed softly. 'Perhaps is it I who needs to teach you some romance.' Then he pulled her into his arms, and his mouth was on hers, and her whole world turned to flame.

He'd once been her friend...now he was a king and her husband, and they would have a family. They would bring healing to this country, *their* country.

They would bring healing to each other.

It was the happy ending she'd always longed for, yet never quite dreamed would be hers, and now it was. And all because of a vow she'd written on a stained serviette, one night in a bar in Soho.

Once, she'd thought that getting him to sign it had been the stupidest thing she'd ever done.

Now she knew it was the best decision she'd ever made.

EPILOGUE

KHALIL LOOKED OVER the crowded ballroom to see if he could spot his beautiful wife.

Everyone was here for his marriage celebration ball and his staff had outdone themselves. Sidonie had insisted it be in the throne room because that was where they had been married and also because the tiles were beautiful. He'd agreed, and so now his throne room was full of light and music and people laughing. Exactly as he'd hoped when he'd first come to get Sidonie from England a month earlier.

She had taken to being his queen like a duck to water, helping him to organise the redistribution of wealth to his populace, drawing on her charity and management experience in order for the whole process to run smoothly. And it did.

Her charity, too, was making waves in Europe, helping disadvantaged children everywhere, and soon they would be launching it in the States, with a fundraising ball planned in New York at Christmas.

Managing her new role as Queen with her charity commitments was a big job, but Sidonie was an excellent manager of both her own time and other people's, far better than he was. Already she had every single person in his court eating out of her hand.

Galen and Solace had a little crowd of people around them, while Augustine kept checking his watch and looking irritated. Apparently he was waiting for Freddie, his personal assistant. She'd got delayed in London by something and wouldn't be back until much later.

Cool fingers suddenly gripped his.

Khalil frowned and turned, only to find Sidonie's green eyes looking back at him.

She was magnificent tonight in the green gown she'd had especially designed, an off-the-shoulder number that laid bare her pale shoulders and with sweeping silken skirts. And gleaming in the hollow of her throat was the delicate little golden sunburst necklace he'd presented to her just before the ball had started, in reminder of a very private, very personal memory they shared. She'd cried and he'd kissed away her tears.

His breath caught at her loveliness.

'What is it?' he asked.

But she only smiled mysteriously and pulled at his hand, drawing him over behind one of the pillars, where it was quieter.

'What, *ya hayati*?' Sudden concern tightened inside him. 'Are you well?'

Sidonie's smile was radiant. 'I'm well. I'm very well.' Then she closed the space between them, put her hands on his chest and rose up on her toes. 'I'm also very pregnant,' she whispered in his ear.

He didn't know what it was that went through him, a lightning strike of emotion that rooted him to the spot. And then, as her lips brushed his ear, he understood.

Happiness. It was happiness.

'Sidonie,' he whispered back. 'My sunshine. You make me so very happy.'

He'd thought his heart was made of stone until she'd taught him his mistake.

It wasn't made of stone.

It was made of love.

There was no doubt at all in his mind.

* * * * *

If you were enchanted by
Her Vow to Be His Desert Queen,
*then you'll love the first instalment in
the Three Ruthless Kings trilogy,*
Wed for Their Royal Heir

And look out for the final instalment,
Pregnant with Her Royal Boss's Baby,
coming soon!

*Why not also dive into these other stories
by Jackie Ashenden?*

Pregnant by the Wrong Prince
The Innocent's One-Night Proposal
A Diamond for My Forbidden Bride
Stolen for My Spanish Scandal
The Maid the Greek Married

Available now!

#4121 THE MAID MARRIED TO THE BILLIONAIRE
Cinderella Sisters for Billionaires
by Lynne Graham
Enigmatic billionaire Enzo discovers Skye frightened and on the run with her tiny siblings. Honorably, Enzo offers them sanctuary and Skye a job. But could their simmering attraction solve another problem—his need for a bride?

#4122 HIS HOUSEKEEPER'S TWIN BABY CONFESSION
by Abby Green
Housekeeper Carrie wasn't looking for love. Especially with her emotionally guarded boss, Massimo. But when their chemistry ignites on a trip to Buenos Aires, Carrie is left with some shocking news. She's expecting Massimo's twins!

#4123 IMPOSSIBLE HEIR FOR THE KING
Innocent Royal Runaways
by Natalie Anderson
Unwilling to inflict the crown on anyone else, King Niko didn't want a wife. But then he learns of a medical mix-up. Maia, a woman he's never met, is carrying his child! And there's only one way to legitimize his heir...

#4124 A RING TO CLAIM HER CROWN
by Amanda Cinelli
To become queen, Princess Minerva must marry. So when she sees her ex-fiancé, Liro, among her suitors, she's shocked! The past is raw between them, but the more time she spends in Liro's alluring presence, the more wearing anyone else's ring feels unthinkable...

HPCNMRA0623

#4125 THE BILLIONAIRE'S ACCIDENTAL LEGACY

From Destitute to Diamonds

by Millie Adams

When playboy billionaire Ewan "loses" his Scottish estate to poker pro Jessie, he doesn't expect the sizzling night they end up sharing... So months later when he sees a photo of a very beautiful, very *pregnant* Jessie, a new endgame is required. He's playing for keeps!

#4126 AWAKENED ON HER ROYAL WEDDING NIGHT

by Dani Collins

Prince Felipe must wed promptly or lose his crown. And though model Claudine is surprised by his proposal, she agrees. She's never felt the kind of searing heat that flashes between them before. But can she enjoy the benefits of their marital bed without catching feelings for her new husband?

#4127 UNVEILED AS THE ITALIAN'S BRIDE

by Cathy Williams

Dante needs a wife—urgently! And the business magnate looks to the one woman he trusts...his daughter's nanny! It's just a mutually beneficial business arrangement. Until their first kiss after "I do" lifts the veil on an inconvenient, inescapable attraction!

#4128 THE BOSS'S FORBIDDEN ASSISTANT

by Clare Connelly

Brazilian billionaire Salvador retreated to his private island after experiencing a tragic loss, vowing not to love again. When he's forced to hire a temporary assistant, he's convinced Harper Lawson won't meet his scrupulous standards... Instead, she exceeds them. If only he wasn't drawn to their untamable forbidden chemistry...

YOU CAN FIND MORE INFORMATION ON UPCOMING HARLEQUIN TITLES, FREE EXCERPTS AND MORE AT HARLEQUIN.COM.

HPCNMRB0623

Get 3 FREE REWARDS!

We'll send you 2 FREE Books <u>plus</u> a FREE Mystery Gift.

FREE Value Over $20

Both the **Harlequin® Desire** and **Harlequin Presents®** series feature compelling novels filled with passion, sensuality and intriguing scandals.

YES! Please send me 2 FREE novels from the Harlequin Desire or Harlequin Presents series and my FREE gift (gift is worth about $10 retail). After receiving them, if I don't wish to receive any more books, I can return the shipping statement marked "cancel." If I don't cancel, I will receive 6 brand-new Harlequin Presents Larger-Print books every month and be billed just $6.30 each in the U.S. or $6.49 each in Canada, a savings of at least 10% off the cover price, or 3 Harlequin Desire books (2-in-1 story editions) every month and be billed just $7.83 each in the U.S. or $8.43 each in Canada, a savings of at least 12% off the cover price. It's quite a bargain! Shipping and handling is just 50¢ per book in the U.S. and $1.25 per book in Canada.* I understand that accepting the 2 free books and gift places me under no obligation to buy anything. I can always return a shipment and cancel at any time by calling the number below. The free books and gift are mine to keep no matter what I decide.

Choose one: ☐ **Harlequin Desire**   ☐ **Harlequin**   ☐ **Or Try Both!**
                        (225/326 BPA GRNA)   **Presents**   (225/326 & 176/376
                                                                            Larger-Print   BPA GRQP)
                                                                            (176/376 BPA GRNA)

Name (please print)

Address   Apt. #

City   State/Province   Zip/Postal Code

Email: Please check this box ☐ if you would like to receive newsletters and promotional emails from Harlequin Enterprises ULC and its affiliates. You can unsubscribe anytime.

Mail to the **Harlequin Reader Service:**
IN U.S.A.: P.O. Box 1341, Buffalo, NY 14240-8531
IN CANADA: P.O. Box 603, Fort Erie, Ontario L2A 5X3

Want to try 2 free books from another series! Call 1-800-873-8635 or visit www.ReaderService.com.

*Terms and prices subject to change without notice. Prices do not include sales taxes, which will be charged (if applicable) based on your state or country of residence. Canadian residents will be charged applicable taxes. Offer not valid in Quebec. This offer is limited to one order per household. Books received may not be as shown. Not valid for current subscribers to the Harlequin Presents or Harlequin Desire series. All orders subject to approval. Credit or debit balances in a customer's account(s) may be offset by any other outstanding balance owed by or to the customer. Please allow 4 to 6 weeks for delivery. Offer available while quantities last.

Your Privacy—Your information is being collected by Harlequin Enterprises ULC, operating as Harlequin Reader Service. For a complete summary of the information we collect, how we use this information and to whom it is disclosed, please visit our privacy notice located at corporate.harlequin.com/privacy-notice. From time to time we may also exchange your personal information with reputable third parties. If you wish to opt out of this sharing of your personal information, please visit readerservice.com/consumerschoice or call 1-800-873-8635. **Notice to California Residents**—Under California law, you have specific rights to control and access your data. For more information on these rights and how to exercise them, visit corporate.harlequin.com/california-privacy.

HDHP23

HARLEQUIN
PLUS

Try the best multimedia
subscription service for romance
readers like you!

Read, Watch and Play.

Experience the easiest way to get
the romance content you crave.

Start your **FREE TRIAL** at
<u>www.harlequinplus.com/freetrial</u>.